A COSTA RICAN CAPER

A NOVEL BASED ON ACTUAL EVENTS

To Ginger,
Thank you so much
for all your guidance on
this.

Steve Venghaus

STEVE VENGHAUS

Registered with United States Copyright office. July 18, 2006.
registration number TXu 1-311-920

Lulu Publishing Services rev. date: 06/19/2014

Acknowledgments

——————————— ■ ———————————

There are a few people whom I'd like to thank for their help on this work: First off, I need to sincerely thank my Brother, Walter who inspired me at a very young age to appreciate and enjoy reading. He later became my sounding board on various authors we had both read. Thanks, Wally. To the wonderful Gringos in Costa Rica without whom this story would have never been told. Thanks Vegas Bob, Pidd, Henry, Donny, Dave, Steve and even you, Norbert. Special Thanks to Bill Edwards who encouraged me thoughtout our five years in that beautiful country. Thanks to my wonderful Sister in law, Linda Venghaus who spent countless hours with her red pen correcting and editing. Also to my friend, neighbor, and fellow author, Roberta Taylor who gave me invaluable advise on this project. A special thanks to all the wonderful people of Costa Rica, a country I truly fell in love with. Finally to my friend, Ginger Herold for without your patience, hard work and understanding, this work would have never seen the light of day.

Pura Vida!
Steve Venghaus
Las Vegas, Nevada

Contents

Acknowledgments...v

Chapter 1   Frank 1

Chapter 2   Arrival In Paradise 5

Chapter 3   Wally... 10

Chapter 4   Vito And Marvin 16

Chapter 5   Dick Banks 20

Chapter 6   The Del Sol 25

Chapter 7   Fun In Paradise 31

Chapter 8   The Cousins 33

Chapter 9   Back To New York.......................................36

Chapter 10   Early Summer In San Jose 41

Chapter 11   Call For Help 44

Chapter 12   The Pitch..47

Chapter 13   Back To Paradise...50

Chapter 14   The Meeting..54

Chapter 15   Journey's End..57

Chapter 16   An Idea...59

Chapter 17   Recruitment...62

Chapter 18   Settling In..66

Chapter 19   Dinner 68

Chapter 20   More Recruiting 70

Chapter 21   The Final Meeting 75

Chapter 22   A Plan Comes Togeater.................................78

Chapter 23   A Bus Ride To Nicaragua 80

Chapter 24   A Change In Plan..85

Chapter 25   The Doc..88

Chapter 26   The Ops Plan 92

Chapter 27   Jump Traning 96

Chapter 28   Jump Off..100

Chapter 29   On The Island 105

Chapter 30   Journey To Liberia 112

Chapter 31   Scrubs..116

Chapter 32   Packing Up...120

Chapter 33   The Procedure 123

Chapter 34   12,000 Feet Up 129

Chapter 35   Escape From The Island...132

Chapter 36   Lost At Sea 136

Chapter 37   Safely Home...140

Epilogue..143

---■---

CHAPTER 1

FRANK

Frank Sommers was dozing and was not aware that the fast moving jet had begun its initial descent into San José City, Costa Rica. Frank was dreaming about this, his first vacation in over five years. A few hours ago, after knocking off the last of his airline lunch, he treated himself to a Baileys and then put the too narrow coach seat back as far as he dared and nodded off. It was in this state that he thought about his work as a transportation business journalist working the same beat at The Shipping Journal for the past 15 years. He loved writing but he loved traveling more. Sure the paper gave him assignments where travel was involved but going to cover conventions in Cleveland or Des Moines was not his idea of exotic travel.

Due to staff shortages, a messy divorce and college tuition for his son, Billy, to attend Columbia, he had no choice but to work as much as possible - like non-stop for the past 5 years, putting all his exotic travel plans on hold. All he could do was drool over the travel brochures he would get from the travel desk at the paper.

About four weeks ago, he was called into John Grimes' shabby, small and drab office. Grimes was his editor and because of Frank's seniority, he and John got along fine. John liked Frank for a lot of reasons, the main one being that Frank never gave him guff and accepted any and all assignments. John, dressed, as always in his standard dark blue suit and spit shined shoes started out by making small talk as he always did and then out of the blue John said, "I wanted you to be the first to know. The Journal has been bought out. An

English group called the Financial Digest paid the old man handsomely for this rag."

Frank just looked at him with shock in his eyes. John went on "I can tell by the way you're looking at me that you're concerned and that's why I called you in. From what I've been told, they will have a transportation news page and I get to keep one reporter. You're it, buddy. Now, it's going to take some time for the due diligence and what not to go through. I'm sure that once it's through, all bets for employees who stay on will be off, which brings me to my next subject: How many vacation weeks you got coming?"

Frank muttered something about 4 weeks or so.

John said, "Ok, that's what I thought. Just so you won't lose it when the new group takes over, I want you go back to your desk right now and fill out a request for four weeks' vacation. I'll push it through and you can be on some beach by next week.

Frank said, "Are you sure? You're not pulling my leg are you?"

Grimes laughed and said, "No Frankie I'm not. After this goes through, I'll need you like never before and I want you as rested as possible."

Frank told him Ok and went back to his desk to ponder what he just heard. By hook or crook, he had managed to put a little money aside and as he gazed out his office window, all he could see was the cold, gray downtown New York scene offering nothing but other office buildings full of workers doing much the same work he was doing. Christmas had come and gone with Billy off on a ski vacation with college buddies leaving Frank feeling very depressed and lonely in his one bedroom Hoboken walk up. What the hell, here's a chance to do something for me. For the first time I can remember, I've got the money *and* the time.

Once he had decided on a getaway, Frank was torn as to where to go. Being a divorced male, he thought about all the exotic and hedonistic vacations his imagination could muster up. Bangkok, the Philippines and Single Cruises crossed his mind. Frank had heard from bragging single guys that all of these destinations were famous for beautiful and willing girls. Sex was now almost non-existent because ever since he had lost his girlfriend of 3 years in the World Trade Center disaster almost 18 months ago, he could no longer muster up the will or energy to go back on the dating scene.

He then thought back to that day: It was a beautiful September morning. The temperature was in the mid-sixties with a azure sky. He had a spring in his step as he walked toward the big twin towers. He had finally secured an early morning interview with John Larson, the Port Authority's shy and withdrawn Maritime Director. Until now, no one had been able to secure an interview with Larson. Frank persisted and was always polite and eventually he had softened John up enough for him to agree to a short interview. The date was Tuesday, Sept. 11, 2001. Frank was happy because his editor, John Grimes would be very impressed and who knew? He might even get a scoop.

Life was good, he thought. With that sophomoric thought in his mind, he walked into the lobby of Tower 1 and just as he did, he heard what he thought was a freight train and then the whole building shook. People froze and just looked at other people for some kind of explanation. Then everyone started running outside. No hero, Frank joined them and found himself on the street looking up and realizing something terrible had happened. Others pushed him and he went along with the flow. About a block away, he finally stopped and looked up at what had to be the 90th something floor where he saw red and yellow flames billowing out.

"Oh, My God" a lady nearby shouted, "A plane crashed into it!"

Frank like everyone else was stunned. Then he heard sirens and a policeman was telling everyone to move north. Frank did as he was told. About a block later, he froze as he remembered that Marion, his girlfriend of 3 years worked as a bond trader for Stuart and Osley in the second tower. Another policeman told him to move.

He looked at the cop and said "My girlfriend works in Tower 2".

The cop said "Don't worry, they started evacuating Tower 2. Everyone will be fine, just move on, you'll hook up later."

Reluctantly, Frank continued walking north. It was just a few hours later that he realized she couldn't have made it. The second plane had most likely hit her floor direct or just below it. God, he missed Marian. She was intelligent, good looking and great in bed. He was still dozing when his mind shifted yet again and he remembered about a call he had received from an old friend who had recently retired and moved to Costa Rica. He had told Frank about the beautiful weather, countryside and relatively low cost of living in Costa Rica, not to mention the beautiful women who were crazy about anything American, especially old retired gringos with money. The way his friend, Wally Phillips, described it, there was no downside. Frank had immediately got on his computer and discovered that it was relatively cheap to go there - especially when compared to some other destinations he had looked at. In addition, Bangkok's flight time from Newark airport would be 17 or 18 hours, while Costa Rica was a mere 5 hours south of Newark. The more he looked, the more Frank became convinced that on his limited budget, Costa Rica was the only exotic destination he could afford for his newly acquired vacation. He reached for the phone as he looked for Wally's number. After a brief conversation, Wally had even offered to pick him up at the airport and show him around. Not a bad idea Frank thought. Besides, he hadn't used his high school Spanish for 30 years.

CHAPTER 2

---◾---

ARRIVAL IN PARADISE

S uddenly, he felt the back of his seat being pushed up. The cute Latina flight attendant was telling Frank (in Spanish) that the plane was landing and all seat backs and tray tables must be in their upright position, *'Por favor, Señor.'*

As he rubbed his eyes, he looked out the window and saw lush green rolling hills and mountains and the red tile roof tops of small houses with dirt road driveways leading to one lane blacktops. The whole panorama was enhanced by a cobalt blue sky with puffy white clouds scattered here and there. He thought, not bad, Frank, it looks awful nice. But where was the water and the beaches strewn with bikini-clad chiquita's he had heard so much about? Then he remembered he was landing in San José, the capitol city of Costa Rica and that San Jose is located in the central region of the country - some 2 hours by car east of the Pacific ocean and 5 hours west of the Atlantic. Then he recalled reading that Costa Rica is located on the isthmus between North and South America, bordered to the North by Nicaragua, to the south by Panama, to the west by the Pacific Ocean and to the east by the Caribbean Sea. The country is about the size of West Virginia and home to one of the oldest democracies in the Americas.

Then the 737 dropped altitude and wheel gear at about the same time and Frank felt it speed up as the pilot adjusted attitude, lowered the flaps and lined up for his final approach. Moments later, he felt a thud as the jet touched down and then heard the powerful reverse thrust of the engines as the Captain slowed the now grounded vehicle in order to make a hard U-turn at the end of the short runway. As they taxied to the gate, the flight attendant announced that they would have to go through customs here in San José and welcome to Costa Rica.

After waiting in line for what seemed like an hour, Frank was waved right through when the agent saw that he was obviously a gringo *tourista*. After recovering his bag, Frank went outside to a storm of hungry taxi drivers all shouting to him "taxi, taxi". In the back, he spotted the familiar face of his friend, Wally waving to him. Frank made his way through the crowd and reached out to shake Wally's hand noticing right away that the button down figure of Wally Phillips, once a CEO of a major transport company, stood before him looking like the biggest Jimmy Buffet fan Frank had ever seen. Wally had put on at least 50 lbs. since retiring and was dressed in flip-flops, a Hawaiian shirt and cargo shorts.

Frank grabbed Wally's outstretched hand and said: "Wow, you look great" a little too sincerely.

Wally just smiled and said "Welcome to paradise, amigo."

Frank, dressed in a white shirt, slacks and blazer looked a little out of place and his face showed bewilderment. Wally, noticing this, said "lighten up, amigo, you're on vacation." Wally then turned to a short, dark good looking Costa Rican (Tico) standing beside him and said, *"Miguel, este es mi amigo, Señor Frank y el esta en la ciudad de San José por dos sermanos."* (Miguel, this is my good friend, Frank, and he will be joining us in San Jose. For two weeks)

Frank stood open mouthed as the overly friendly Miguel pumped his still outstretched hand saying in perfect English, "Welcome to my country, Senor Franco. Let me take your bag". With that, he turned and headed to a red Kia taxi with Frank and Wally in tow.

Once on the Autopiesta that led from the airport to the city of San José, Frank said, "Wally, you came to pick me up in a taxi?" Wally laughed and told him that owning a car in Costa Rica is very expensive due to the Costa Rican government's tax regulations which, coupled with the high cost of importing a car, can easily double the cost of the car had it been bought in the US.

Wally explained that most ex-pats living in the confines of the San José area simply take a taxi wherever they go. "Taxis run the equivalent of about .60 cents per trip. It's too expensive to have a car and, even if you do, it'll probably get stolen unless you have a house in a gated community. Owning a car is just plain dumb. Even the gringos that live outside the city just take busses which run every 5 minutes and are even cheaper than taxis."

"Wow, looks like you've got it figured out," Frank said.

"That's not the half of it, amigo," Wally said. "You can live here on the cheap even if your sole income is only a social security check."

"No way", Frank said.

Wally chuckled and simply said, "You'll see amigo, you'll see".

The ride from the airport to San José took about a half hour and offered a view of coffee plantations, high-rise hotels and entrances to industrial parks well off the highway. Half of Costa Rica's three million population reside in *"Chepe"*, as the locals refer to their beautiful city. The route they traveled was part of the Pan American Highway, which can take you from Alaska all the way to South America. The part that runs through Costa Rica is well paved and considered safe - unlike some parts that pass through Nicaragua or San Salvador which features military check points with soldiers pointing AK47's in your ear as they search you, looking for money and/or bribes.

The particular stretch they were on resembled parkways found in the New York/NJ area, which was not at all unfamiliar to Frank. Miguel was a good driver and he negotiated the traffic well. Miguel was a typical tico. He was married with a son and he worked very hard to support his young family. This Kia was a major investment for him. He was proud of it and it showed. While almost a six-year-old car, the Kia looked almost new. Miguel worked on it himself every spare moment. He was an "independent" which meant he didn't work for a company. The money he made was his to keep. He made a good salary - about $90.00 a week, which is considered a good wage in Costa Rica. Like most cars in Costa Rica, it had a stick shift and Miguel was adept at shifting through the gears thereby saving the brakes and expensive trips to the repair shop.

Miguel was making a left and Frank noticed that the main street they were now on boasted car dealerships, hotels and even American chain restaurants. The street was full of taxis, trucks and busses. Private cars were rare and the few that you spotted were either Korean or Japanese. Because of the high cost of car ownership, a top of the line Kia or Toyota was considered a luxury car.

The further they went, the denser the buildings became. Car dealerships and restaurants yielded to a mix of office buildings with retail shops on the first level, government buildings, department stores and more hotels.

The hotel that Wally had arranged for Frank was called the Gran Hotel, Costa Rica. This 83-year-old hotel was a national landmark. In its heyday, it was considered the finest hotel in the country. There is a plaque outside proclaiming that John Kennedy had stayed there in 1962. The architecture alone is something to behold. It sits proudly off the *Plaza Cultural* adjoining the beloved Theater National, another San José landmark, along the famous Aveneida Segundo in the heart of the business and government center of the city. As the taxi pulled up, Frank saw that this grand structure had obviously fallen upon hard times. While not totally run down, the aging six-story building was starting to show its true age. In spite of this, it was still a sight to behold with its sidewalk café just outside the main entrance and its white portico beckoning travelers and hungry diners alike. The Plaza Cultural is alive every day with vendors, tourists, shoeshine boys, beggars and locals meeting other locals with handshakes and hugs. There is a saying that if you stay in this plaza long enough, you will run into everyone you ever knew in Costa Rica. If you need to meet someone in San Jose, this is where you arrange to meet. There are plenty of benches to sit on while you wait for your *amigo* or *amiga*.

Frank and Wally got out of the cab. They were immediately surrounded by vendors offering deals on everything from butterfly art to Cuban cigars. Wally just smiled and forged ahead while Frank took the time to listen and look, which caused Miguel to grab Frank's arm as he walked by with the bag. Once inside, he was surprised to see that in order to get to the reception desk, they had to walk through a full-fledged casino offering everything from blackjack and roulette to old-fashioned style "one armed bandits". Once at the desk, he was greeted by a lovely tica who gave him a smile that made him feel welcome and flattered him at the same time. Wally said something in Spanish to the girl and the way she smiled at him, Frank thought she had to be flirting. He would later learn that it's just the way between men and women in this wonderful country.

Wally said, "Frank, my Man, you're in good hands. The bellboy will take you up. Freshen up and come down when you're ready, Miguel and I will be at one of the tables over there". Wally pointed towards the casino.

Frank, still a little awestruck, muttered something about "Ok, sure" and reached in his pocket for his credit card as the girl was asking to take an imprint.

■

CHAPTER 3

WALLY

Wally Phillips crossed the lobby, entered the casino area and went up to his favorite pit boss, Bernardo and stuck out his hand greeting him with a hearty *"Buenos amigo, como Está?"* Bernardo smiled and greeted Wally like a long lost brother, pulled out a chair for him while snapping his fingers for the Senorita who would get Wally and Miguel something to eat or drink while they played Wally's favorite game of Tute, which is unique to Latin America. Tute is much like Caribbean Stud but has subtle differences. Like Caribbean Stud, the player is given 5 cards and his poker hand must beat the dealer but the dealer has to have at least an Ace and a King or better in his hand to qualify to play. If the dealer doesn't qualify, the player just gets paid on his "ante" bet, which is also known as the front-bet. In order to play, the player puts up an ante and, if he gets what he thinks is a good hand, he backs up his ante by doubling it in the back. In addition, he can bet a bonus bet of up to 500 colones. A bonus bet is paid on dealt straights and above. Should you get dealt a Royal Flush, you would receive the "Accumalado" which can be as high as 25 million colones (about $48,000). Wally loved playing this game, which requires a lot of luck, and Wally was one lucky guy.

Wally Phillips came out of the Army in 1966 with no idea how he was going to support himself. Yes, he could have stayed in the Army but since he was an infantry "ground pounder", that would have meant a tour in Vietnam and, since he was "accident prone", he didn't like that option. So he passed on the three thousand "re-up" bonus and headed back to New York to make his fortune.

Over drinks with an old high school buddy, he heard that United Airlines might be hiring. The next day, he took a bus to JFK and found United's personal department in an old hangar near the entrance to the large airport. The personnel guy was very impressed that he had made sergeant in such a short time (two years) and offered him a position as an agent in their airfreight department. Wally, needing a job, readily accepted without even knowing what airfreight even meant. Two weeks later, he found himself at the airline's training center at Chicago's O'Hare airport. They taught him about tariffs and gave him customer service skills. While there, they put him up at a local motel, which also housed numerous girls who were in stewardess training school. Being fresh out of the Army, young and in good shape, he attracted quite a few young fillies from the Midwest who were awestruck by their newfound positions and not to mention freedom. Wally thought that he had landed the best job in the world and had a ball while in training. The time went all too fast and before you could say *"Jack Robinson"* he was back in New York, with the alarm ringing in his small Queens apartment. It was his first day of work at United's JFK cargo facility. As he put on his new uniform, he realized that he was changing Army green for United blue. For some strange reason, this caused him to chuckle as he hurried out of his apartment and went to the corner to get the bus to JFK. He got off in a warehouse area and found United's cargo facility located in building 82. He reported to the office and asked for Art, the only name he'd been given. The receptionist, a cute little Italian girl, smiled and called, "Artie, da new guy's here".

"Sounds like I'm expected," Wally said with a smile, which was eagerly returned by his new admirer. A gruff looking guy who emerged from behind a closed door interrupted his flirting.

"You Phillips?" Art Taylor asked as he approached the desk.

"Yes Sir", was all Wally could come up with.

Taylor replied, "You can cut the Sir crap, this ain't the frigging Army. I'm Artie," he said as he stuck out his hand.

For some strange reason, they hit it off and in the coming months and years, Taylor showed Wally everything he knew about his passion which happened to be United Air Lines and more specifically, the Air Freight Department of same.

Taylor was a good teacher and Wally was a fast learner. He learned about the office work including customer service and operations. Out on the dock, he learned about how the business operated from the ground up. He unloaded planes, stored freight in its respective area and dealt with the truckers who would show up to pick up freight that had been consigned to them. He was good at it and, like Taylor, he grew to love the work. After work, he would have a few beers with the guys and flirt with the young girls from customer service in a local bar that catered to airline workers. Many a night, he would wind up taking one of them back to his little Queens apartment.

He was happy with his life and his job. The airline treated him well. He was able to use the travel privileges, which allowed him to see much of the country including California, which he especially liked. It was the 60's and free love and the golden tans of the California girls drew him out there with an ever-growing frequency. Then came the blizzard of '67 and he got snowed in at the airport for three long days. His car was buried in five feet of snow and once it was over, he vowed that he would get a transfer to California by hook or by crook. It turned out to be harder than he had thought. Just about everyone who worked at United wanted to transfer to California.

He had been waiting and waiting when he met a guy at the local bar who told him that his company, an air freight forwarder, was getting ready to open a Los Angeles office and he knew for a fact that they would love to get a hold of a guy with Wally's experience to work for them out there. Wally thought about what the guy had told him for about two weeks before he sought him out a week later and got an appointment with the Regional Vice President at their JFK office.

Feeling a little like a traitor, he met with the man whose name was Bill O'Brien. O'Brien turned out to be a no nonsense type who was all business at work but after work he was just another hard drinking Irishman who loved to party. O'Brien grilled Wally for almost two hours and then stunned Wally by saying, "when can you start?"

Wally sat there dumbfounded before asking "start what?"

O'Brien gave him a half smile and said, "The management training program. You'll be reporting directly to me and the salary is eight hundred a month. How's Monday sound?"

Since he was making just a little over four hundred, Wally readily accepted. From that point things moved quickly for Wally. He showed up at the offices of Airborne Freight on Monday and was told to go home and pack a bag, as he and O'Brien would be flying out to Los Angeles that afternoon. Upon arrival in LA, they were met and taken to a luxurious hotel near the airport. In the week that followed, Wally learned that twelve-hour days were common for O'Brien, which left him little time to look around for a place to live, but he did manage to find a place close to the airport that he could afford. He put a deposit down, flew back to NY and was back three days later to move in. Work dominated his life in the coming years but he learned fast and his responsibilities grew faster.

Within a year, he was the Los Angeles District Manager and on the fast track for future promotions. The company liked him. They told him to get a passport and within a short time, he was traveling all over the world meeting with would be agents to team up with Wally's fast growing firm. Since he spoke three languages, he was asked to travel more and more which he did. He became a Vice President and somehow found the time to settle down with one girl whom he had met at work. They had met and married within three months. They were childless which never bothered Wally as he was always immersed in work. Work became a passion and Wally was good at it but there was something else nagging at him and one day while traveling back from an extremely difficult assignment, he realized that he could do this himself. He had amassed some money. Going against all odds, and all advice, he left his secure future with Airborne and started his own freight company. In the beginning, it was just him, his wife, and a good friend who had faith that Wally could pull it off.

One by one, his accounts came with him. He negotiated good deals with the airlines to carry his customer's freight, followed up on everything and slowly but surely, the company grew. Unfortunately, his personal life suffered and before long he was offering his wife of 17 years a divorce settlement. After the divorce, he once again immersed himself in his work and stepped up the pace. He opened offices all around the country but when he went international, it cost him his health. After suffering a stroke and being told by his doctors that if he continued his stressful corporate lifestyle he would be dead in six months. His partners reluctantly bought him out at the relatively young age of 55.

Through his business travel, he knew that Costa Rica offered a quiet lifestyle, good weather, plenty of chichas (women) and, most of all, he could afford to live much better there than in the states on his new pension. Wally loved, in no particular order: gambling, women and food. In Costa Rica he had all three, every day. He had never been happier. He had found a small but nice one bedroom apartment in a good area of the city for a mere $350.00 a month, he had a maid who came in once a week, went to a different favorite *resturante* at least five nights a week, not to mention his girl friends who right now numbered three. The only stress he had was making sure these three, who lived in different parts of the city never bumped into each other. With his computer, he kept in touch with all his old business cronies who came down frequently to enjoy the wonders of Costa Rica and catch up on old times with Wally. One such crony was Frank Sommers, the transportation reporter with whom Wally developed a strong business relationship, not to mention a good friendship over the years.

Wally felt a tap on the shoulder and there stood Frank all bright and shiny from his shower and freshly dressed in T-shirt and shorts. Wally thought 'all we have to do now is get this boy a tan and he'll fit right in.'

Since Wally knew that Frank didn't gamble, he tipped the dealer and cashed in for about 3,000 colones more than he had bought in for.

He told Miguel, *"Buena suerte, amigo, Hasta luego."* He got up and said to Frank, "Let me buy you a cup of coffee". They went outside to the sidewalk café, which adjoined the hotel. They took a table that offered a good view of the plaza, not to mention the beautiful women walking to and fro. Frank noticed that other customers included tourists and a good amount of older white men sipping coffee, reading and talking. The tourists were easy to spot with their tans, knapsacks and hiking boots.

The old white men were another story. They were all over 50, spoke Spanish fluently to the passing girls and seemed to know one another. Now Frank was asking Wally, "who are these guys". Wally told him they were all ex-pats mostly American and a few Canadians. They meet here every day to drink coffee, discuss world events and flirt with the girls. Frank just sat back and took in the scene. He was starting to understand why Wally chose this place to retire.

He was brought out of his trance by Wally who was asking how long he would be here. "Two weeks. But I wish it was two lifetimes." Frank said.

Wally laughed and gave Frank a light punch in the arm saying, "Now you're getting it, the first time I came down here, I was in awe of the place. The hardest part for me was leaving. I mean, I had the damnedest time getting on the plane to go home and believe me, I've never felt that way about anyplace before. I usually can't wait to go home from a trip. I just flat out fell in love with the country, the people, the weather, everything and I didn't even speak Spanish very well back then. After my first fix, I made some 25 trips back before deciding to retire here."

Frank had a faraway look on his face, perhaps because of what Wally was saying and perhaps because of the scenes going on around him. The vendors, tourists and locals all had one thing in common: they were smiling and looked happier than any group he had ever seen in New York. He said, "Wally, why does everyone look so happy and content?"

Wally looked around for a moment, turned back to Frank and said' "They call it *Pura Vida.*"

"Come again?" Frank said. "It means the good life, *amigo.*"

Wally went on, "This country has something that no other place on earth has and I think it's more of a sense of ease than anything else. Ex Pats, like me and a lot of other guys I know are obviously happy - we have money and are much better off than the average tico, that's how we refer to native Costa Ricans, ticos, but it's more than that. I know people here who don't have a pot to piss in but they're happy. Why? The weather? No. I think it's the feeling of contentment that you have here." Frank said, "What does that mean?"

"Well it's hard to put your finger on but I think it's got something to do with there aren't any military targets here, and there is no threat of nuclear war."

Frank interrupted, "Wait a minute! Nuclear war would affect the entire world." Wally shot back, "Yeah but the difference is that you and I know that, but they don't. Frank, as long as they have their rice and beans and the good weather and a warm woman, they're happy. It's the old ignorance-is-bliss theory and it's alive and well here."

CHAPTER 4

---■---

VITO AND MARVIN

"**H**ey Wally, been to the Del Sol lately?" a considerably older looking man sitting at the next table said with a heavy Brooklyn accent.

"You bet I have, Vito, and, if I'm not mistaken, Marvin, Dick, and you were hitting on some fine chicas there yourselves," Wally said with a smile on his face.

"Guilty, Señor," Vito, who was having coffee with Dick and Marvin said. Everyone chuckled and went back to their coffees.

Wally turned to Frank and said, "Those guys are typical ex-pats. They came down here for a vacation, were so awestruck by the women, climate and cheap living, they decided to stay. I see them here all the time having breakfast. They all have one thing in common, they are all investors in The Cousins, a high interest paying investment scheme firm that has offices right over there." Wally pointed to one of the shops located along the hotel's side covered portico. Frank asked how these guys had wound up here.

Wally took a deep breath and said, "OK, Vito, the guy with the Italian knit shirt trying to look and act like Tony Soprano, is really a butcher and sometime bookie from Brooklyn. After his divorce about 3 years ago, he became convinced his ex had turned him into the IRS for not declaring his bookmaking income. So one day he decides to sell his business, car and co-op in Howard Beach, took him about two months but he scraped together about $100K. He had no ties, and had heard that Costa Rica won't extradite for income tax evasion, which is wrong but he doesn't know that. He hops a flight down here to look around. He gets here, checks into a hotel, meets some beautiful tica who smells the money, gets an apartment and he moves her in. He's like a kid - does it every day, sometimes twice. As an ex-New Yorker, he used to go to Atlantic City on a regular basis, so it's no surprise that he discovers the casinos here and now he spends all his time with girls, gambling, or checking on his investments."

Frank said, "Hmmm, not bad. I guess he's set, if you're into that sort of lifestyle."

Wally replied that Vito's story wasn't all that unusual. Frank asked about the others. Wally said, "OK, See the old fart with the white shoes, fishing hat and Sears catalogue pants? That's Marvin. Nice enough guy. Couple, three years ago, he's living with Esther, his wife of 40 years, in a retirement village near Ft. Lauderdale. One day, they're taking a stroll on the walking path near their 2-bedroom cottage and Esther stops, takes a deep breath and falls on the pavement. Marvin yells to passersby to call 911 and starts giving her mouth-to-mouth. Darn shame, she's DOA at the Emergency Room. He's devastated. Four months after the funeral, he's still walking around like a mummy. His friends in the community fear that if they don't do something, he would most likely follow Esther to the hereafter. They convince him what he needs is a vacation.

They all chip in and with the limited money they raise, all they could afford was a one-week package deal to sunny Costa Rica. When he reluctantly leaves, he's still comatose but when he gets here, he discovers that the hotel the cheap travel agent booked him into is the Del Sol." Frank interrupted, "Isn't that the place Vito was just kidding you about?" "Yeah", Wally said, "It is. And you know what else? It's a whorehouse. Not the kind you're thinking of but every night, the bar fills up with 50 to 100 beautiful 19 to 25 year old hookers. I'll tell you more about that later. Now, where was I?"

Frank said, "You were telling me that Marvin's travel agent booked him in there."

"Yeah, that's right", Wally said. "Ok, now Marvin sees these girls in the lobby and is absolutely dumbstruck. Never in his sheltered Jewish life has he seen or experienced anything like this! Beautiful women were coming up to HIM and flirting with HIM. Now, as you can see, Marvin is no George Cooney. Hell, he's not even a George Burns! Well, Marvin comes out of his self-imposed trance, once the old juices start to flow, and he has the most incredible week of his life. He can't get enough and he's blown away at his ability to perform, with the help of a little blue pill he can buy here for a fraction of what it costs in the States. For a 67-year-old guy, he's amazing. The week flies by and now it's time to go home. He goes through what all first time Costa Rica male visitors go through: He doesn't want to go. He is practically forced into the cab by the hotel staff. He thinks about bailing out of the cab on the way to the airport but reality wins out and he goes back. When he gets back, he immediately puts the retirement cottage on the market. It sells in three days. He has a garage sale and practically *gives* his possessions away - even the golf cart. Anyway, he too nets about a hundred grand, takes the first flight back here, gets an apartment, and settles into the good life after investing half of the hundred with the Cousins."

"The Cousins, huh, how much interest do these guys get"? Frank said.

"Fasten your seat belt Frankie, almost three percent".

"Three percent! That's not so hot." Frank said.

"Not per year, Frank, per MONTH!" Wally shot back.

"Not possible," Frank said.

"Possible and probable buddy," Wally said. "Another thing, they've been doing it for over two decades."

"What? What's the deal, Wally? Is it bonds, stocks, exchange rates?"

"No one knows for sure," Wally said. "Everyone speculates about drugs or money laundering. No one's certain but who cares, they pay the monthly interest like clockwork."

"Well do they have a prospectus?" Frank said.

Wally chuckled and said, "Hey, man this is Latin America, not the states. Prospectus, ha, that's a good one." Wally said as he gave Frank an arm punch. "Seriously, when pressed, the Cousins say that they invest the money in hard working Costa Rican companies that need the capitol for equipment needs. You know - factoring, but that's all they say. Most of the investors, like these guys and me, don't really care - just as long as we get our payment every month - in cash I might add.

"Whew!" Frank said as he thought about a possible story for the new financial paper he now worked for. For a moment, he just looked at Wally and the three retired gringos in the background, noticing the last one: good looking, tan and well - dressed in a 1980's sort of way. Then Frank said,

"What about him?' pointing to the very young looking retiree sitting with Marvin and Vito.

"Oh, you mean Dick Banks. He's a story unto himself, Ex-Army, Special Ops. Some say he worked closely with the CIA too. He retired about 4 years ago. Came straight here. Never even considered anyplace else. A lot of ex-military live in Costa Rica. Anyway, he's an investor too."

CHAPTER 5

———————— ■ ————————

DICK BANKS

The year was 1968 and 18-year-old Dick Banks was sitting in a South Vietnamese rice paddy, his face covered with mud. He was tired, but he couldn't sleep. He had to stay awake and alert. He knew they were coming and he had to be ready. His squad had set up the ambush and now came the hard part: waiting, which gave your mind a chance to wonder. What the hell was he doing here in the first place? Dick thought. It seemed like yesterday, he and his buddies were terrorizing the suburbs of Jacksonville, stealing cars for joyrides with the inevitable babes that would join them for a few beers and a ride in a new convertible. It was great, Dick remembered. Nobody messed with him and his gang. He was the bad boy and the girls fell all over him. Everything was fine until the night when they ran low on beer and someone suggested holding up the package store. They left the car running while they went in and pulled a knife on the little Puerto Rican clerk. They quickly grabbed what they had come for. One of them cold cocked the Puerto Rican and they ran out the door. Right into the hands of the waiting cops who had spotted the stolen car from the street.

The Juvenile hearing judge was a tough cookie, and he dispatched the cases quickly. Dick saw two of his buddies sent to the JV detention camp. The judge, a throwback to the old days, took a look at Dick. He must have seen something in him because he offered Dick a choice. Two years in Juvenile detention camp or a stint in the Army. Both Dick's parents and the lawyer advised him to take the Army. Not having much of a choice, he chose the Army.

He was too impulsive for his own good he thought. Then he thought back to the time in basic when the spit and polish looking sergeant from the 82nd Airborne had come through the barracks yelling something about them all being candy-ass ground pounders if they didn't go Airborne. Airborne? He thought. I wonder what that's all about. The Sergeant went on calling them play soldiers and pussys and finally saying that he was leaving and if there was one man amongst this bunch of candy-asses, he should go with him. Impulsively Dick and two others sprang from their bunks. The Sergeant was elated and took them in the day room to brief them and sign them up for jump school.

After a quick leave when he completed basic, Dick reported to Fort Benning, Georgia, where they taught him how to jump from one foot, three feet, 20 feet, and then a tower of 100 feet. He thought he had known how to fall but they taught him that too. He learned to hit the ground and turn his body in such a way as not to get hurt. They also taught him how to be one tough son-of-a-bitch. He got cockier as each day went by and when he finally made his first jump and realized that he loved it, he was officially a paratrooper in the meanest, baddest fighting division in the US Army, the 82nd Airborne.

Dick looked the part in his bloused boots, rakish garrison cap with the airborne insignia and the silver jump wings on his chest. When he went home for another quick leave before reporting for deployment to Vietnam, the bad boy turned paratrooper got more than his share of girls. Then as fast as it had begun, his leave was over and he reported to Travis Air Force Base in California for deployment to the Republic of Vietnam.

Reality sunk in as the big 707 dropped to 10,000 feet over Saigon and began its rapid anti-aircraft evasion decent into Saigon. It was late 1967 and he almost passed out in his class A's as he stepped out of the cool air of the plane and into the brutal afternoon humidity of South Vietnam. After doing paperwork, getting combat gear and a one-day orientation, he was choppered to the field to join his unit, Charlie Company of the 1st Battalion, 3rd Brigade. Charlie Company held the high ground in an ungodly place called Chu Lai and unbeknownst to all of them, Tet was about to begin.

Now night was falling and he could feel bugs and God knew what other creatures crawling on his face, neck and hands. He peered through the twilight to locate his buddies. They were all half submerged in the rice paddy waiting for the VC.

Minutes and then hours passed and suddenly they heard the low roar of a truck running along the paddy. Everyone in the patrol got the signal from the squad leader and crouched down with the exception of the grenadier who readied his M79 grenade launcher. Then Dick heard the pop of the grenade being launched, and the sky lit up. He stood up to fire at the escaping troops. The ambush had evidently worked as everyone around him fired and soon the road was strewn with black pajama clad-bodies.

Before they could congratulate each other someone yelled "incoming" as they simultaneously heard the whine of mortar shells coming from the sky. Dick ate mud as he dove into the trench alongside the road. Shells were exploding all around him as he lay in the mud. He heard screams of pain and yells for medics. He was convinced this was the end. Just then, the shelling stopped and Dick peered out to see an armored troop carrier approaching. "Oh Shit, he muttered, they're coming to finish us off." Dick looked around to see if anyone else had spotted the approaching vehicle and for a moment he thought he was the only one left. Then he heard a loud whisper saying, "Banks, you see that?" Dick muttered, "Yeah" to the yet unseen voice. The whisper turned out to be Peterson, the squad leader.

Peterson then told him he had been hit and it was up to Banks to scramble along the trench, get behind the carrier and, as it stopped lob a grenade into the back just as they opened the ramp. Dick thought Is this guy crazy? I'll get killed, but something told him to just do it and without another thought, he was off scrambling along the ditch like a lizard. Somehow, he managed to position himself just to the left rear of the vehicle as it came to a stop, he pulled the pin and threw the grenade unnoticed by anyone in the carrier. Bang! Dick looked up as smoke and fire billowed from the open hatch and ramp. Instinctively he ran out of the ditch firing his M16 from the hip. It was then that he noticed that these were no ordinary VC's. These guys we clad in the uniform of North Vietnamese Regulars. The NVA were battled hardened troops not to be taken lightly. Although he didn't know it, TET had begun. Dick hit the ground and just as he landed, he felt a sharp pain in his arm. At first, it felt like a bee sting, and then he felt warm blood running down his arm. "I've been hit," he said to himself as the pain became more pronounced. Then out of the corner of his eye, he saw movement in the shadowy night and realized that the surviving members of the NVA patrol were moving in to finish him off. With his good arm, he raised his weapon and started firing. He got the first one but the other one was moving and firing back. Just as he squeezed off another round, he felt a hot sensation in his neck and everything went white.

He awoke to the whoop, whoop, whoop of a chopper engine and realizing that he was on board, he looked up to see a bandaged up Peterson looking down at him. He raised his good arm and was restrained by an IV line, which was hooked up to it. "Stay down, Banks, they're taking us to a MASH unit. You're gonna make it."

"What happened, Sarge?" Dick said through clenched teeth.

Peterson laughed and said "What happened is that you saved the whole patrol is what happened, man. Now rest." Peterson pushed him back down. Then blackness overcame him as the morphine worked through his system.

Later, he woke up in a hospital room. He had no way of knowing that he was on a hospital ship off the coast of South Vietnam. His arm and head hurt like hell, but the Doctor was telling him that he'd be ok and that it was probably a ticket back to the states. He spent the next week on the ship recovering and was just about to be choppered back to Saigon so they could transport him to the states when some General and a couple of other officers came by his rack to pin medals on him. One turned out to be the Silver Star, which was given to him for saving the patrol. Something he had no idea he had done. The General was saying something about "With total disregard for his own safety, Private First Class Banks, continued attacking the enemy while protecting his comrades." Evidently, everyone but him had been wounded in the mortar shelling. Had the troops in the armored carrier been allowed to exit, his buddies would have been slaughtered where they lie.

After his recovery period, he was given some leave time and told to report to Ft. Bragg to some Major who turned out to be a Special Forces officer who wanted to recruit Banks for his unit. Since he liked the Army and wanted to make a career of it, he didn't need much convincing. He was sent to training at Bragg, then the Language school in California where he perfected Spanish and Vietnamese then special weapons school in Maryland. Upon completion of his training, they promoted him to Buck Sergeant and then sent him back to Nam where he did two more tours over the next 3 years.

Banks spent a total of 30 years in the Army, most of them with Special Forces (now Special Ops), and saw service in Panama, Nicaragua, Columbia, The Gulf and Bosnia.

He retired to Costa Rica, a place he had gone to for R&R over the years. He had been exposed to Costa Rica during the Iran Contra problem. It was the R&R destination for his group during the skirmishes with the Contras and the Somosa government. Costa Rica and its people was, in his opinion, the most peaceful environment he had ever found. It was also the only place he could afford to retire on his meager pension.

He had made a minimum investment in the Cousins about 2 years ago and had met Vito and Marvin in the office while collecting his monthly interest. While 15 years their junior, he felt comfortable with these two and enjoyed their conversations over breakfast. Since he had lost his Dad to the Korean War, he looked upon the two retirees as father figures. Like Wally, he enjoyed the tables in the casinos but was limited because of his stipend. He had a comfortable "tico" house near the university and he never tired of looking at the young co-eds walking by as he sat on his porch and waved. He had a cute 27-year-old girlfriend who was always talking about marriage but he was having too much fun for the time being. Dick had stayed in remarkable shape and appeared to look more like 35 than his real age of 51, which kept the girls very interested.

The waiter came by and said, *"Mas coffee, Senor"* to Wally who waived him off and asked for the check. He looked at his watch. They had been talking for two hours and now the early dinner crowd was starting to arrive.

Frank yawned, and Wally said, "You've had a long day and I'm making it longer. Sorry buddy."

"No, no, no, Wally. I just need a little break."

"Ok," Wally said looking again at his watch. "Why don't you take a nap for a couple of hours and then we'll grab a bite and go to the Del Sol to check out the action." Frank agreed and the two rose. Frank went up to his room and Wally went back to join his friends at the tables.

CHAPTER 6

THE DEL SOL

Wally was just about to cash out when he saw Frank walking towards him. He got his money, said, *"Yo voy"* to the group and ushered Frank out the door and into the early evening on the plaza. Frank started towards the taxi stand and Wally grabbed his arm saying, "Where're you going, Man?" Frank looking a little confused said, "Didn't you tell me to take a cab after dark?"

Wally replied, "Ok, ok, you learned well but if there are two of us and one of us knows the safest way, it's ok to walk. I didn't mean to scare you. There are lots of areas that are safe to walk at night and this is one of them."

Now they were on a big promenade that took them past boutiques, fast food places, department stores and small hotels. The walkway was bustling with office workers hurrying to get home. There were street musicians, beggars, and artists all around. The general mood was cheerful as people were talking and smiling at one another. They walked about three blocks and took a left that took them uphill. Frank saw a huge seven-story pink and white building at the end of the block with a neon sign on top proclaiming "Hotel Del Sol" and said to Wally, "That it?"

Wally said, "You bet, buddy. Brace yourself." Frank thought, what the hell is he talking about, it can't be that good.

Three gringos who had come to Costa Rica some 11 years ago owned the hotel. All three were entrepreneurs with experience in the restaurant, bar and hotel business. They had heard about a large (by Costa Rican standards) 55 room hotel in the center of downtown for sale. Although the place was fairly rundown, the three saw a potential so, realizing they would have to do an entire renovation, offered half the asking price. To their amazement, the offer was accepted. The next two years, they sweated, worried, and worked to get it in order. Labor was relatively cheap and they were able to rent a few rooms during construction which helped get them through. One of them was very computer orientated and knew how to market it to other gringos back in the states. When they added a casino and bar, they got their own Website and used the power of the Internet to their advantage. Americans, hearing about Costa Rica's beautiful women flocked to San José. Word soon spread that the Del Sol was the place with the hottest girls. The girls had come because the Gringos had come. With them, the Gringos brought money and the girls could smell the money. Pretty soon, they expanded, adding more rooms plus penthouse suites for themselves. Pura Vida had taken hold for them. Sure they continued working hard but work was fun and they enjoyed providing a service that Americans could never get back home.

Without a word, they made their way through the front door and Frank took in the expensive Mexican tile floor, the casino dead ahead, and the huge front desk off to the right with a small coffee café to the left. Behind the casino area was an elevated bar with a railing that overlooked the casino area. Frank noticed the stuffed sailfish mounted over the bar that accounted for the name of the saloon, "The Blue Sailfish." Then he noticed that most of the patrons in the crowded bar were girls. Then he saw that all of the girls were beautiful and were dressed in sexy, revealing outfits that left little to the imagination as to what was beneath.

Frank didn't realize it but he had stopped in his tracks. His jaw was hanging open and he had a faraway look in his eyes. Wally poked him in the arm and laughing said, "Gotcha Frank". Frank was too engrossed to reply but Wally forged ahead, "Your reaction is typical. Every newbie I bring in here has the same look on his face that you have right now."

Frank muttered "O Man, is this heaven?'"

Wally chuckled and said, "Not quite, but it's pretty close"

Just then, one of the girls came running up to Wally saying, "*Hola, Senor Wally, mi amor.*" Then switched to English saying, "Wally, why I no see you here lately? I miss you, *mi amor.* You want some me tonight?" As she was saying this, she was running her tongue around her voluptuous lips causing Frank to blush.

Wally, turning a little flushed himself said, "Juanita, my love, *come esta, tu?*"

Juanita answered by rubbing his chest, stomach and started reaching down further when Wally took her hand, brought it to his lips and kissed her hand extravagantly. Juanita swooned and said, "Wally, you make me so hot."

Wally coughed and gestured towards Frank and said, 'Juanita, this is my *muy bueno amigo, Sr. Frank Sommers.'* Juanita looked Frank up and down and said," Señor Frank, I am very pleased to meet a friend of Señor Wally, thank you very much.". She was obviously showing off her good English.

Frank smiled and, in return got the sexiest smile back he had ever seen. The three of them chatted for a while and then Juanita took Frank by the hand and led him up the stairs to the bar area. Once there, she started introducing him to all of the other girls. When Wally saw that a couple of them had sat down at a table with Frank, he joined them. One with bleached blonde hair, dressed in designer jeans and a top that covered little, was sitting on Frank's lap. Frank looked happy and confused at the same time.
Wally said, "I see you've met Lucia." To which Frank just nodded. Lucia was rubbing his thigh and licking his ear simultaneously. Frank was aroused and Lucia was giggling. Then she said in broken English, "Where you hotel Francisco." Frank said something about the Gran Hotel Costa Rica to which Lucia pouted and said, "Mucho far but I have hotel just around corner"."

Wally interrupted, "She's talking about the Hotel Asia, it's a by-the- hour place that they all use. Be sure to get the price out of the way before you go with her." To which Frank muttered, "How much?" Lucia immediately spat out, "'one hundred dollars." Wally shook his head holding up five fingers.

Frank got the message and said, "Fifty dollars." Lucia once again went into her pouting act to which Frank said, "Ok, sixty but not a penny more." Lucia smiled, stood up and grabbed his hand starting to walk away. Frank resisted and looked at Wally, who said, "Go ahead, that's a good deal. You won't regret it. I'll still be here when you get back. Look for me at the tables."

Frank smiled at his friend, then looked at Lucia and said' *"Vamanos"* with his poor Spanish accent. Lucia giggled and off they went. Juanita looked at Wally and said, "Your friend is too horny, he could have had her for fifty."

Wally laughed and said, "Give him a break, honey, it's his first time. He'll learn."

When they got to the hotel, Frank was a little disappointed. It looked like a dive. Once inside, Lucia did all the talking and soon he found himself in a small room with a mattress on the floor taking up most of the room. Off to the left, he saw a small bathroom with a stall shower. Lucia was saying, "You shower?" Frank, now confident said, "Only with you." She smiled and started taking her clothes off. The top took about two seconds and revealed to him that her wonder bra had been working overtime but it didn't matter to him because he was more of an ass and leg man anyway. Very quickly, she stood before him completely naked. His mouth dropped open. She asked with a little pout, "You no like".

Frank said, "I like, I like" as he closed his open jaw. She was at least a nine and she told him she was 19. Since there weren't any stretch marks, he thought she might really be that young. She slowly walked over to him and started kissing his cheeks, ears and mouth. Then she put her hand inside his shirt while using the other hand to massage his crotch. He was immediately aroused and before he knew it, she was un-zipping his fly. He pulled her up and said, "Shower." She smiled and went into the small bath to turn on the water. As she bent over, he saw a perfect ass and said "Whew" to himself as he rapidly removed the rest of his clothes.

In the shower, she started lathering him up and rubbed him everywhere. He was in a trance. What a beautiful body, he thought. And she's with me and she obviously wants me. Now it was his turn to explore all of her nooks and crannies, which he did. Now she was moaning as his hands found her beautiful butt and crotch. He was breathing hard so she turned off the water and reached for a towel and began drying him. They were half done when they fell on the mattress. He was all over her with his hands and tongue. Meanwhile, he had grown erect so she pushed him back while positioning herself between his legs kissing his stomach, thighs and crotch. Now Frank was moaning as she looked up and pointed to his member and said, "You want me here?" All he could mutter was "Si, por favor". She smiled and immediately devoured him. His eyes rolled back into his head and he was breathing hard as she slowly and deliberately worked up and down. Afraid that he might cum, he gently pulled her to him and she complied by rubbing her wet clit against his manhood. Then she rose and using her fingers, inserted him into her moist crevice. She was moving slowly as he watched her small but beautiful breasts bounce in his face. His lips grabbed one and she moaned more. Now they both moved up and down in unison and before he knew it, he had exploded inside the condom that he didn't even realize she had slipped on him. Aaaaah, he moaned, as did she too.

Later, they cuddled and his hands wondered all over that beautiful body. Even though a hooker, she was happy and content to lay with him as long as he wanted. While dressing, he handed her the agreed upon fee plus another $20.00 for excellent service. She was very grateful and showed it by kissing him passionately on the lips, then took out paper and pen and wrote her phone number down saying, "You call me and we can have fun again, no?"

Walking hand in hand, they entered the Del Sol, which had thinned out considerably. He immediately spotted Frank at the tute table and waved. Noticing that he was anxious to see his friend, she said something about joining her friends, and gave him a big wet kiss and hurried up the stairs. He stood motionless for a moment watching that beautiful ass retreating up the stairs. Then he remembered where he was and almost tripped over a table full of drunken gringos as he walked over to Wally.

"How was it, dude?' Wally said with a smile.

"Oh my God, where do I start?" Frank said.

Wally laughed and patted him on the back saying, "Easy boy, easy, Remember you've got a week to go here. What you just experienced is normal down here. Nine out of ten are exactly like her. I hope you brought your little blue pills."

"You gotta be kidding. Nothing I ever had in the states was like that," Frank said.

Then Wally said, "These girls are the best and the cheapest in the world. I've talked to guys who've been to Bangkok, Columbia, the Philippines and Japan. No place can compare. It's like I was telling you before, it's the contentment that everyone seems to possess here. Either they really enjoy it or they're the best actress' on the planet. Plus, $60.00 is a lot of money to these girls. The average worker doesn't make that in a week!"

'Wow, I didn't realize that but it's the best $60.00 I ever spent." Frank said.

Wally smiled as he turned over 5 spades that paid him 60,000 colones because he had placed 300 colones on the top bet. "Now, that'll get me three sessions with Lucia, Eh?" Frank shook his head and said, "Wally, you are one lucky dude."

Looking at the dealer, Wally replied to both saying, *"Surete Gringo, Eh?"* The dealer smiled and thanked him as Wally threw him a 5,000 colones chip.

"What's next?" Frank said as Wally gathered up his chips and rose.

"What's next is dinner, I don't know about you but I'm starving." Wally said.

Frank was happy to hear that as he had worked up quite an appetite.

CHAPTER 7

FUN IN PARADISE

The next ten days, Frank and Wally played "tourista" and visited famous beaches, volcanoes and resorts all around Costa Rica. They went to Puntarenas to catch the boat to Tortuga Island where they snorkeled in crystal clear water, laid on the beach, and swam in the warm tropical water. Two especially memorable days were spent at the famous Aranal Volcano where, along with Lucia and Wally's current *favorita*, they frolicked in the hot springs and at night gazed up at the erupting volcano while soaking in the hot water. Later, back in the rooms, they both enjoyed the pleasure that the girls were all too willing to provide. They met for breakfast the next morning. Wally pulled out a map and asked if anyone wanted to go horseback riding. The girls screamed with delight so Wally pulled out his cell. He contacted the Lodge office and made arrangements to go to the *finca* (farm) later that morning.

The horseback riding turned out to be one of Frank's most memorable times in Costa Rica. Wally's horse turned out to be the oldest and biggest of the bunch. He needed a stool to mount the big gelding and even with that, he required assistance from the guide. Frank and the girls were having a good laugh at Wally's expense. The horse must have appreciated the attention, for at that moment he took a leak with most of it winding up on Wally's leg. At this the girls laughed so hard that *they* almost peed themselves. It was in this spirit that they started out on a trail that afforded them the most beautiful scenery Frank had ever seen. As they rounded bend after bend, they were treated to artistic landscapes with the big Volcano serving as a backdrop. At one point, as they were moving though a pineapple field, the guide dismounted and expertly cut a pineapple with his machete. He handed everyone a slice and Frank couldn't remember a pineapple that ever tasted so sweet.

After they left Aranal, they went on to the beaches of Jaco and Manuel Atoinio where they frolicked in the surf. Frank got terrible sunburn. Later in their room, Lucia spread lotion on him. The site of her nakedness naturally aroused Frank. Seeing this, Lucia took care of his other needs. In spite of the pain caused by his sunburn, Frank thought he was in heaven.

Every night, they went to a different restaurant. If nothing else, Wally knew where all the best ones were. Near Puntarenas, they found a place situated on a river that fed into the ocean. This restaurant featured a delicious fish called corvina that was similar to sea bass. All the fish served here had been caught by local fisherman who caught them on the restaurant's pier. The chef would come to your table and you would pick out your own. When the fish arrived, Frank's first bite told Wally he had made yet another good choice.

On the way back to San Jose, they made a stop at the Laz Paz Waterfall Park. Wally had arranged rooms for them at the famous Peace Lodge, which offered rooms with breathtaking views of the waterfalls. The price of the room included a tour of the 5 tiered waterfalls. They walked down all five and went through the butterfly atrium where they saw exotic butterflies that are unique to Costa Rica. At the bottom, they were met by a bus, which took them back up to the top where the hotel lobby was situated.

The girls enjoyed the fantastic rooms, which even included hot tubs. Not accustomed to such luxurious surroundings, the girls were more obliging than usual when they retired to their respective rooms. Frank just wished the fantasy the place offered lasted longer.

When they returned to San Jose, the fun continued. They drank, gambled and partied with the girls. Frank had never experienced a vacation like this and he dreaded the day he would have to return.

He had called his editor a couple of times and his inner mind told him all was not right. Grimes wasn't telling him everything and Frank knew it. He was not all that excited about leaving paradise for the problems that awaited him in New York.

CHAPTER 8

———————— ■ ————————

THE COUSINS

It was the night before Frank's departure for Newark and Wally had taken Frank out for a last meal at his favorite steak restaurant, the La Palma in the Bario Amon section of San Jose. The La Palma is famous for its Argentinean meat, which is nothing less than succulent. After ordering, Frank took a sip of wine and questioned Wally how the cousins got started.

"Well Frank, it's a long story," Wally said.

"We've got all night," Frank replied.

"Ok, Mr. Reporter, I'll tell you. The principal Cousin, Senor Enrique Hernandez was born in Golfito to a very average middle class family. Golfito is southeast of here, down near the Panama border. Today it's kind of a duty free area where many locals go to buy major appliances. They actually run bus trips from San José. To get the duty-free price, you have to stay overnight, but the savings are huge and a lot of people go down once or twice a year. Anyway, young Enrique or Ricky as he is known was a dreamer. He loved aviation and he would hang around the hangers at the local airport cleaning helicopters for the owner of a small shuttle service. He was very tech minded and after a while, he was trading his salary for flight lessons. He was a quick study and learned well. The instructors and the owners respected him. Eventually, he convinced the owners they could make more money spraying crops when the helicopters were not in use at night. They liked the idea and before anyone knew it, he was running a very lucrative side operation for them. He now made more money than anyone in this family had ever made. He was constantly trying to improve the operation and one day got into a heated argument with the owners over the allocation of fuel for his operation. In the end, the owners fired him. Not one to grieve much, Ricky headed north to Nicaragua and got contracts with growers in that country. Armed with the contracts, he then convinced the Somosa government-controlled banks to finance him and he purchased two used helicopters and started his own crop dusting company up there."

"Sounds like quite a success story." Frank said.

"Yeah, well wait until you hear the rest." Wally uttered.

"Next thing you know, the Sandinistas make a move on the Somosa government and before you know it, our young entrepreneur's venture is taken over by the Sandanistas. Ricky gets out with his life and some capital, comes back to Costa Rica and dammed if he doesn't form another aviation firm and then go right back to the same banana growers he used to service, and asks them to help him get started."

"Don't they have any tort laws here?" Frank asked.

"You keep forgetting that this is Costa Rica, Frank. Tort laws don't mean much here."

"Oh, yeah, I see. What happened next?" Frank asked.

"Well the business thrives. As a matter of fact, he drives his former company under and before you know it, he's the only helicopter service in the county. Has like 30 choppers serving the growers, tourists and government."

"Yeah but that doesn't sound like an investment scheme", Frank said.

Wally drew a deep breath and went on, "Like I said, he does real good. Makes a lot of money. He buys villas, fancy cars and expensive clothes. After a while, he's bored. While looking for something for his cousin, Memo to do, he notices that Costa Rica has a thriving black market money exchange business going. He sees locals changing money for tourists outside the Post Office every morning. He supplies Memo with cash and they start competing with the other exchangers. Everything Ricky touches turns to gold and before you know it, he and his cousin own the largest money exchange operation in San Jose. From that, they move into lending money to American Ex Pats and make good profits. From there, it isn't much of a stretch to go into the factoring business. Many of his helicopter clients are in a seasonal business and they need funding to get them through the lean months. Ricky is all too willing to help and makes a tidy profit off the interests on that too. One day, he and cousin Memo are talking about how they can offer even bigger loans for the larger coffee industry and they come upon the idea of offering high interest, like 26 or 27% per year to the gringos, then loan the money out to large Costa Rican companies for 36%. They take the plunge almost 25 years ago and the rest, as they say is history, my friend."

"Whew, this guy is a regular Horatio Alger." Frank said.

"You bet, man. He sure is well liked by us Ex Pats. He pays like clockwork. I get a calendar every year and the days that I pick up my interest are shaded each month on the calendar. Don't forget, it's paid in cash."

"Man, what a deal. Listen, I've got a small savings account up north, can I get in?"

"Sure, but you have to be referred by a current client. I'll be happy to introduce you whenever you want." Wally told him.

"Ok, let me get back to you as to when I'll be coming back," Frank said.

CHAPTER 9

BACK TO NEW YORK

A nagging pounding on his hotel room door rudely awakened Frank. His head was throbbing and the sound wasn't helping. "Who is it?" he yelled.

"Frank, it's Wally with my friend Miguel who's here to take you to the airport." Wally Phillips answered.

"Oh my God! What time is it?"

"Nine o'clock, good buddy. You have exactly two hours till wheels up."

"Oh shit. Give me a second." With that he pulled on a pair of pants and opened the door, told them to have a seat and ran to the bathroom. Thirty minutes later, they were heading north out of the city towards the airport.

Wally, ever happy was chatting up a storm. "We're gonna miss you, good buddy. Did you have a good time? I hope so because now, you've got to go back to that button-down world up north."

"Yeah, that's right good buddy, make me feel good." Frank muttered from the back seat.

Wally laughed and said, "Come on, it ain't that bad."

"It sure is. I hate to leave. This place is paradise."

"You're experiencing what all of us have gone through. Right now, you're probably thinking about how you can get back as soon as possible."

"Guilty." Frank said.

Now they were pulling up to the curb and as Miguel jumped out to get Frank's bag out of the trunk, Wally started hugging him and now Frank was thinking about how and when he'd come back. They said their goodbyes and Frank worked his way through the various checkpoints and found himself sitting in the boarding area waiting for his row to be called.

As they took off, Frank looked out the window at the green hills and fading landscape and vowed to somehow return to this new paradise he'd discovered. During the flight, he dozed in and out thinking about Lucia, the beautiful country he had just left and the story about the Cousins his friend Wally had told him last night. Knowing that he was now working for a paper that's main focus was finance, he wondered whether or not he should discuss the Cousins and the potential story with Grimes. In the end, he decided to hold off and save it for just the right moment.

The big jet touched down at Newark without incident and he moved through baggage claim and customs with ease. Outside, he caught a taxi and found himself walking up the stairs to his 3rd story walkup apartment in Hoboken two hours after he had landed at Newark. Tired and knowing that he had to go to work in the morning, he collapsed on the bed and was out before he hit the pillow. Maybe it was the time difference but he woke at 4:00 Am and had plenty of time to unpack, and catch up on the mail before getting ready for work. Struggling with his tie, he already missed the casual dress he had grown accustomed to in Costa Rica. He thought about Wally who had probably just woke up, pulled on a pair of shorts and slipped on flip flops and would now be on his way to the outdoor café in front of the Gran Hotel. Lucky bastard, he thought as he completed the knot and watched his neck turn red in the mirror.

Catching an earlier train than usual, he found himself at the office a full half hour earlier than usual. He walked into his office and was surprised to see a woman sitting at his desk. "Hi", was all he could muster.

The sign on her desk proclaimed that she was Ellen Barkly, Assistant Editor.

She looked up and said, "Can I help you, sir?"

"I'm Frank Sommers."

Puzzled, she looked at him and said, "And?"

Frank said, "And a couple of weeks ago, this was my office"

"Oh my God, you're *that* Frank Sommers," she said.

At that moment, Grimes was walking by and seeing Frank standing in front of the desk, he made a quick detour into the room. "Frank! How are you? When did you get in? Didn't you check your messages at home?"

"What messages?" Frank almost yelled.

"Frank, let's go to my office," Grimes said touching Frank's arm.

"Yeah, sure, John, let's go to your office since I obviously don't have one," Frank shot back as Ellen's face reddened.

Once in his office, Grimes shut the door and strode to his chair saying, "Sit down buddy, hey, how about a cup of coffee? Water?" Pressing the intercom, he yelled "Connie, get us some coffee in here, please!"

Grimes looked at Frank.

In return, he got a cold stare, then Frank said, "What the fuck is going on, John"

"Now don't get upset, Frank, the new owners had their own executive staff and we found we had to do a little shuffling. We've ordered cubicles for everyone who's been inconvenienced. They've made huge improvements in office systems, I'll think you'll be impressed. They're almost like small offices. Really quite nice."

"Yeah, right, quite nice. Just give it to me straight, John." Frank said.

"Ok, Frank, I guess I owe you that much." Grimes sighed, "The good news is that you have a job. They don't think a lot about transportation, but I was able to convince them that transportation companies do have annual reports and do file chapter elevens and seven's. I wanted you to have a page but they would only agree to a daily column."

"A column!" Frank blurted just as Connie entered the room with a tray of coffee, which she almost dropped when she heard Frank's eruption.

"Just leave it over there," Grimes said pointing to a side credenza. Connie placed the tray down and almost ran out of the room. "Yes, a column, Frank. It was the best I could do. Maybe when they see what you can do, they'll come around and I can get you more. In the meantime, it's all I can do. They are really focused on the world financial picture." From the look on Frank's face, Grimes knew that he wasn't convinced, but he went on anyway. "Look, Frank, I'm doing the best I can. Things change. I know that you can dazzle 'em with your work. Have faith and I'll keep fighting for you. In the meantime, don't kill the messenger, Ok?"

"Ok, I guess." Frank said. "But I don't like this one bit. Where is my desk? I'd like to see if anything's missing."

Grimes smiled and said, "That's the boy, come with me."

Unenthusiastically, Frank followed him into the big open area and was somewhat pleased to see that Grimes had at least insured him a window. Probably out of guilt, Frank thought. Grimes excused himself while Frank grunted something in return. He checked his drawers, phone, computer and notes. All seemed to be in order. He thumbed through his messages and started organizing them noticing a call back from Roger Curren, the President of CNF Inc., the second largest trucking company in the U.S. Frank had heard that they were having financial problems and he decided to make that his first call.

Waiting for Curren to come on the line, Frank thought about his meeting with Grimes. "Shit", he thought, "This is all I need": He had just blown half of his savings on the vacation and now he felt his job might be in jeopardy. Oh, sure Grimes could protect him but only so much. Financial, financial, financial, he thought. Then he remembered about the Cousins story and he resolved that he would talk to Grimes about it later. He might have something, he thought.

"Frank?" Curren was saying, "That you?"

"Hi Roger, what's up?" Frank mumbled as he came out of his trance.

"Well, I've got some news but first I'd like to know what's going on at your paper. From what I can tell, you're not a transportation oriented publication any longer."

"Yes, that's right but we still have a transport section and I'm handling it."

Skeptically, Curran went on to tell him that his company was about to file for protection under bankruptcy. Frank's antenna went up and he furiously started taking notes on his computer. Why, what, where and when questions flew out of his mouth. Curren patiently answered all his inquiries during the next half hour. Frank thanked him for calling him first and got off the phone as quickly as possible without seeming too rude.

He immediately pressed the intercom for Connie, Grimes' secretary and asked if John was available. Connie checked and told him, a little shakily, to come to the office. He almost ran through the bullpen bumping into a lot of new faces he didn't recognize.

"John, wait till you hear this, I just got off the phone with Curran and CNF is filing for bankruptcy!"

"What?" Grimes said.

"Yeah, Curran's giving me the scoop."

Before Grimes could reply, the phone rang and Grimes picked it up saying, "God Damn it, Connie, I'm in a meeting!" Frank then saw Grimes face lose some color as he told Connie to put the call through. Frank then heard a one sided conversation between Grimes and his new boss, the publisher. "Yes, Sir, I just heard. I've already got a man on it, Frank Sommers. Uh, huh, yes but Frank is my Transportation guy and it's because of his contacts we got the exclusive." Frank noticed that Grimes gave an audible sigh as his jowls dropped visibly. "Yes, Sir. I understand. Ok, I'll get on it right away. Ok, yes Sir. Bye." Grimes hung up the phone and stared at Frank with a blank look.

"*More* bad news, John?" Frank asked sarcastically.

"Oh, Man, sometimes it doesn't pay to get out of bed in the morning. He wants one of his people on it. He wants Ellen to be the primary writer on this."

"No way, John! That can't be. I've known Curran for the last twenty years."

"That's why he wants *you* to work with Ellen on it, buddy," Grimes told him.

"Are you out of your mind? Curren gave me the scoop. Can't you do anything?'

"I wish I could, I'm stuck. Look, help me out on this, Frank. I'll make it up to you somehow."

"Like you helped me out of my office, John?"

Grimes turned red and looked at him saying. "I told you I'm stuck. I can't do a thing. You're going to have to prove yourself all over again."

"Oh, shit." Was all that Frank could say.

Over the course of the next few weeks, Frank bit the bullet and did as he was told all the time reminding Grimes that he owed Frank and he would soon need to collect. Ellen, to her credit, didn't gloat and seemed to understand the situation so Frank was glad to help her. Ellen was a quick study and once the story broke, she insisted sure that Frank got some credit on the by-line. At the very least, Frank had made a new friend. Why not, he thought.

CHAPTER 10

EARLY SUMMER IN SAN JOSE

Wally walked up Aveneida Central enjoying the bright sunny morning. As was his custom, he was headed to the Gran Hotel Costa Rica for breakfast. He was enjoying the sights and sounds and nodded frequently to the chicas he saw every morning on this walk. They smiled, he smiled. Life was good - *Pura Vida,* he thought and quickened his pace as his stomach was now growling.

Being Friday, he stopped to buy a copy of the *Tico Times*, which came out every week on Fridays. Without even looking at the front page, he tucked the paper under his arm and continued on his short journey.

Entering the veranda area of the restaurant, he spotted his favorite waitress who gave him a big smile as she said, "*Hola, Senor Wally. Yo tengo su mesa favorita.*" (I have your favorite table)

"*Gracias, Maria y Buenos Dias, mi amor.*" He shot back in his American accented Spanish while she smiled and blushed.

As he sat, she poured him coffee and asked if he wanted breakfast to which he replied, "*Si, Tostadas Francias y Jugo, por favor.*" (French toast and juice, please) As she moved away, he took a sip of his coffee and opened his paper. The headline changed his jovial mood in seconds:

"**COUSINS OFFICE SHUT DOWN,**" it shouted.

For no particular reason, he looked around to see if anyone was looking at him and then dove into the brief story: It explained that there had been a raid at the offices of the investment firm known as the Cousins and that it was a joint operation of the Canadian and Costa Rican Drug Enforcement Departments. Evidently, one of the Cousins investors was a Canadian who was a known drug dealer and there had been a suspicion of a money-laundering scheme involved. At that point, he looked up and turned around to stare at the office entrance off the plaza. He could make out a small white sign of some sort. He jumped up and almost ran over to the door. Now closer, he could see the sign:

To our customers: This office is temporarily closed and will re-open as soon as possible. The Cousins.

The next sentence was a repeat of the statement in Spanish. He felt his knees go limp and almost collapsed. He felt nauseous as he put his hand over his forehead and peered through the glass door. All the desks, phones and copy machines were there. The lights were out and it appeared that the office was simply closed for one of the numerous Costa Rican holidays. Although he knew it was futile, he pounded on the door and was not surprised when no one answered.

Still weak, he walked back to his table on shaky knees. The food was there but he no longer had an appetite. He sat down and lit a cigarette. As he exhaled the first puff, he spotted Dick Banks, Marvin, and Vito walking across the plaza. As they got closer, he could hear the sounds of quarrel coming from the group. Wally just sat and watched as they approached. As they came up, Wally heard Vito saying, "Goddamn it, Marvin, stop asking me. I don't know anything more than you do." When he spotted Wally, Vito said, "By the look on your face, you know, don't you Wally?"

Wally just nodded his head and pointed behind him with a jerk of the thumb that meant that they should look at the door of the Cousins. Dick made a gesture for Vito and Marvin to stay where they were while he hurried over to look at the sign. While he was gone, Marvin picked up Wally's *Tico Times* and scanned the front page for the umpteenth time that morning.

"Wally", he cried, "what are we going to do?'"

Wally just shook his shoulders and frowned.

Vito muttered, "Fuck it Man, we're screwed"

"Not so fast," Dick said as he strode up. "The sign says it's only temporary. Let's call the main office and make an appointment so we can get the facts before we panic."

"Panic is something I do well," Marvin said as he shook out some kind of medication from a prescription bottle he was carrying with him.

"Let's not jump to conclusions, guys," Dick said. "Obviously both the Canadian and Costa Rican government are involved and right now, they hold all the cards. Look, I've got some DEA contacts from the old days. Let me get in touch and see if I can learn anything. In the meantime, let's just keep our cool and wait to see what the next step is."

Reluctantly, they all agreed. They would watch the paper and try to get more information from other sources and meet here every morning to update each other.

When Dick got home, he grabbed his address book and started making calls. In most cases, he just left messages. Within an hour, he got his first callback from an old Special Ops guy that had gone with DEA when he pulled the pin on the military. Dick had had a good working relationship with his old buddy, John Cummings and for a while, they exchanged information and updated each other. Then he told John about the problem. John told Dick that since it was with the Canadians, he would have to do some investigating and get back to him. "Very good", Dick said and John promised he'd get back as soon as possible.

CHAPTER 11

CALL FOR HELP

At that moment, Wally was back at his apartment considering options. He had come to rely on the $2,000.00 monthly payment he received from the Cousins. It was his mad money, which he used for Chicas and gambling. Without it, he would still be comfortable but he would have to cut back on his vices substantially. Wally loved his life and did not want to have to trim back. Remembering that his friend, Frank now worked for a financial paper, he impulsively picked up the phone and placed a call to Frank's work number. Within seconds, he heard his friend saying,

"Frank Sommers."

"Hi, Frank its Wally down in Costa Rica."

"Wally! It's great to hear your voice." Frank said. "What's up?"

Wally, not sounding like his old self, said, "What's up is there's trouble in River City. You know that investment scheme I told you about?"

"Yes," Frank said a little hesitantly.

"Well, yesterday, they were raided by the Costa Rican and Canadian DEA. They think that the whole thing is a front for a money laundering scheme because a couple of Canadian investors are known drug dealers."

"Oh shit, what's going to happen?" Frank asked as he started taking notes.

Wally, hearing the tap, tap of the keyboard let out a breath and said,

44

"I'm not sure, old buddy. For now, they've closed the office and the paper is reporting that all assets have been frozen pending further investigation by the DEA's of both countries."

"So there's hope."

"I don't know if hope is the word I'd use. Down here these "investigations" take years to resolve." Wally said.

"Man, I'm so sorry. Is there anything I can do?"

"Thought you'd never ask. Now that your paper is concentrating on financial news, I thought you might be interested in covering it. The more the American public knows about it, the more the pressure the government will put on the local boys in blue to resolve this quickly. Tourism is the big business here."

"I see," said Frank as he thought this might be his ticket back to a corner office. During the next few minutes, Frank bombarded Wally with questions about the scheme and its history and about how the other Americans were taking it then he told Wally, that he would make a pitch to his editor and get back to him as soon as he could.

As Wally was saying his goodbyes to Frank, in another part of town, Dick's phone rang. Dick picked it up on the 2nd ring. "Banks."

"Dick, it's John Cummings and I've got some information for you."

"What's up buddy," Dick said as he bit his lip.

"Well, our boys didn't know too much or they did and were keeping it off the radar screen, so I called some of my Canadian contacts and they were almost gushing information."

"Wow, that's good", Dick interrupted.

"I don't know if it good or bad but here's what I found out: Your man Ricky had a lot of well off Canadian investors who are involved with the drug business and the Mounties think they were using the investment scheme to launder profits."

"That meshes with what we know down here".

"This is a big deal for the Canadians and they have every intention of playing it out." Cummings told Dick.

Dick said, "The Canadians are very efficient but the Costa Ricans are very hesitant to act with any swiftness."

"How true, but what can I do to help you?"

"Progress reports, intel on Ricky and his brother would help," Dick said.

Cummings reluctantly agreed and said he would keep in touch. After a few more minutes of reminiscing, they both said their goodbyes.

CHAPTER 12

———■———

THE PITCH

As Dick hung up in Costa Rica, Frank Summers was just sitting down in front of his boss, John Grimes in New York. He had spent the last 3 hours doing research on Expatriates living abroad, The Cousins, Costa Rica and even Wally himself. He was as ready for this meeting as he could be. After explaining the whole story of the investment scheme and how many Americans were involved. John started shooting questions about who, what, when and where. Frank had done his homework and the answers came out as fast as John could ask the questions.

When he was through asking all his questions, Grimes sat back in his chair and stared at Frank to the point it made Frank uncomfortable but Frank just stared back. Grimes said, "First, call the DEA people. I think Ellen may have a contact there. Next, give that Tico Times a call and see what you can learn. Then, try to get some phone interviews with some of the investors. You might also want to try and track down this Enrique guy. I want more information, Frank."

Frank stared at him and said, "Why, so you can give it to Ellen?"

Grimes' face reddened and he started to rise but regained his composure and sat back down. He glared at Frank and said, "I don't like the sarcasm, Frank, but given what's happened, I'll let it pass but just this once. If and it's a big if you have something here, It'll be all yours. Ellen will be there to assist. That's it. Now get to work."

"Yes Sir. Uh, sorry I jumped the gun John. It won't happen again."

Grimes just waved him off but chuckled to himself when Frank left.

The next two days were filled with research, computer searches and numerous telephone calls. Ellen turned out to be a gem. Frank was amazed how quickly she understood the story and he was blown away by how many contacts she had in Washington and Toronto. Grimes had done him a huge favor. Without her help he would have been lost. They worked into the night and through dinner and lunches. Chinese takeout was their constant companion. They managed to get out a good introductory story on the raid complete with background on the Cousins and their disgruntled investors. At Frank's insistence, they shared the bi line. They brought the final copy to Grimes who took his time reading it in his office with the door shut. Finally, he called them both in. They sat down across from Grimes who finally threw the story on his desk and said, "You speak Spanish, Frank?"

Surprised, Frank replied that he was half way through Spanish lessons and was getting better every day.

"I hope they're good enough because I want you on a plane tomorrow." Grimes said.

"Huh?" was all Frank could say. He looked over at Ellen who was smiling.

Grimes said, "Look, I think you've got something here because of all the older Americans involved. Nobody likes to see a bunch of retired folks taken advantage of. You came through. Now I want you to go down there and get me more. I want the readers to see how this unfolds and remember, the old man is watching. I want good research, good writing and prompt reporting. No BS. We don't have the time or the money." Pressing the intercom, he yelled "Connie, book a flight to San Jose, Costa Rica for Frank Summers. First flight out tomorrow morning, coach!" Then, standing he looked at Frank and said, "Get out of here, I've got work to do. And don't let me down Frank. I'm counting on you."

"Yes, Sir" Frank said as he stuck out his hand and shook Grimes's wildly. He then almost ran out of the office as he told Connie that he would be back for the tickets later.

Back at his desk, he started to organize his notes and thoughts. He had to prioritize his work and it took him a good hour. He now had a to-do list. He felt good. The tickets arrived by messenger, true to his word, Grimes had indeed booked him in coach. No matter, Frank thought, I'll be working all the way down and won't have time to relax. He then picked up the phone and called Wally who was happy to hear that he was coming down so soon. Wally told him that to save money, he could stay with him. Frank told him sure and could he have Miguel, the taxi driver pick him up when he arrived tomorrow? "You bet, and I'll be there with him," Wally said. Frank then asked Wally to gather all the information he had on the story including his own original contract and any documents issued by the Cousins since the beginning. He also asked Wally to set up interviews with other investors who had been bilked.

"Tomorrow too soon for you, Frank?" Wally said. Frank chuckled and said, "See you tomorrow morning buddy."

Frank hung up the phone. He had to gather up his notes, say bye to Grimes and get home to pack. He would have to get up early the next morning as the taxi would be picking him up at 5:00AM.

CHAPTER 13

BACK TO PARADISE

N ext morning after touching down in San Jose and clearing customs, Frank walked out into the humid air, true to his word, Wally was frantically waving as Miguel stood next to him with a smile on his face. Quick greetings as they strode to the red taxi he remembered from his previous visit. Once in the cab, Wally, with a grim look on his face, handed him that morning's edition of "*AM Costa Rica*".

"What's this." Frank said.

"Just read the headline, you'll see." Frank opened the paper and right on the top, the headline read: "**One Cousin Arrested, Another Vanishes**"

"Oh shit," Frank said. He then read the opening paragraph:

> *San José. In an early morning raid, local police picked up Memo Hernandez at his Barrio Amon residence and he is now being held under suspicion of drug trafficking and money laundering at the local detention prison on Avenida Primera. Meanwhile, a warrant has been issued for his Cousin, Enrique Hernandes, also of Barrio Amon. When police raided the elder cousin Hernandez' residence, they found no one home. Neighbors state that he loaded up his SUV late last night and left. They speculated that he was going on a vacation. Anonymous police sources suspect that Enrique has fled the country but would not speculate further.*

"Well, I guess I can cross "Interview Enrique Hernandez'" off my list." Frank said with a sigh. "Where we headed?" he asked as he noticed they were going east on 2nd Avenue.

"Interviews with some victims," Wally said.

"Why?"

"There have been stories about suicides, guys selling off all their assets, moving back to the states, all sorts of human tragedies brought on by this."

"Ok, where?" Frank asked.

"At the Gran Hotel Costa Rica, for breakfast. The guys meet there every morning to discuss the latest on this. It'll be interesting to hear what they have to say today," Wally uttered.

"Amen" was all that Frank could say as he went back to the paper. The taxi pulled into the entrance. Wally and Frank jumped out.

Wally looked at Miguel and said, "Wait for us, amigo, next stop will be *mi casa*" Miguel nodded.

As they walked up to the table, they could hear a rather animated conversation going on between Marvin and Vito with Dick acting as a referee. Vito was the first to see them and hollered, "Wally! Tell this schmuck what Ricky's disappearance means, that he took the money and ran!" Dick was shaking his head and Marvin looked mortified.

Wally said, "Look, Vito, I just read the story myself. Let's talk about it before anyone jumps to conclusions."

Turning towards Sommers, Wally said, "You guys remember my friend Frank? Well, he's a reporter for the *Financial Digest* in New York. Frank's an old buddy from my working days and he's going to look into what happened with the Cousins. We can trust him." Surprised looks from the three breakfast buddies, then they all stood, shook hands and made room for the two new arrivals.

After everyone settled, Frank told them he was interested in interviewing them and anyone else they thought might have an interesting slant on the story.

Vito and Marvin were very excited and offered Frank anything he wanted, anytime. Dick just sat in his chair and stared at Frank and Wally. Noticing this, Wally said, "Dick, how are you making out with you former contacts from the Marines?"

"Army, Special Ops, "Dick shot back.

"Yes, I'm sorry. I should have remembered. Anyway, any luck?"

"A little, I got someone checking into it", Dick said with some reluctance. As Wally started to respond, Frank looking at Dick said, "5th Special Ops?"

"Yeah, that's right" Dick muttered.

"Then you speak Spanish" Frank said remembering that the 5th served in Central America.

"Un huh, how do you know about that?" Dick said.

"I was a reporter in Nam - Just after Tet. In Da Nang."

"See any action?" Dick shot back.

"A little, if you count hiding in a ditch when Charlie decided to hit us with his mortar attacks" Frank smiled. Dick kept staring but his eyes softened a bit.

Then Wally said, "Look Dick, we need this story to break in the U.S. It's the only way the U.S. government will put any pressure on the local government here. You're fighting it your own way and this is my way. It couldn't hurt. Think of it as a kind of a two pronged attack."

"I understand. I just don't like being blindsided" Dick said.

Sommers said, "From now on, that won't be a problem. I'll run everything by you before I send it to my editor but I'd like to know what you're doing in exchange."

"I can tell you some, but not everything for now."

"Ok, I can live with that," Frank said.

Over the next two hours, Frank recorded statements from all three. How they got involved, how much they invested, how they first learned of any problems, names of others that might have interesting stories. They also discussed ideas on where Ricky may have fled and with whom. Dick said he had someone on that and he should have more information soon. Wally proposed that they notify as many investors as possible and set up a meeting with all of them so that Frank could interview them all at once. Marvin said he had a list and would make phone calls that afternoon. Vito offered his house as the meeting place. He lived on the outskirts of one the suburbs and that way, they would have privacy and room.

Then they all went their separate ways, Dick to wait by the phone, Marvin and Vito to make calls, and Wally and Frank to get Frank settled in at Wally's place. For the first time in long time, they had a purpose and they felt that they were at least trying to do something.

Before settling in, Frank took out his laptop, hooked it up to Wally's' Internet connection and got off an initial story based on what he had learned that afternoon.

CHAPTER 14

─────────────────■─────────────────

THE MEETING

Marvin's list turned out to be rather complete. In the next few days, Vito and Marvin contacted some fifty other investors. They told them about the meeting and when and where it was to be held. They asked people to notify others they knew who were investors.

Seeing that the number of investors had grown, Wally realized that Vito's house was too small. He contacted a buddy who operated the sports book on the second floor of the Colonial casino. He conned him into letting the investors use it as a meeting place. They had contacted as many as possible and those contacted, called their friends. They were expecting 30 or 40, so when Wally and Frank walked in, they were surprised to see almost 100 sad looking but apprehensive older gringos crowding a room that was meant to hold 50 people. Wally and Frank found Dick, Vito and Marvin sitting near the front and it was Wally who said, "What now, guys." Dick pulled Wally aside and told him that he wasn't very good with speaking and since he (Wally) had some business expertise, could he moderate. Seeing an eager nod from the others, Wally agreed. A table was brought up to the front and Wally directed that five chairs be positioned behind the table. He then asked Frank, Dick, Vito, and Marvin to join him.

With some reluctance, Wally called to the murmuring crowd to order. He started with "Hi everyone. I guess you're wondering why I asked you all here." There was a soft chuckle from the crowd and he resumed with a smile, "Ok, for those of you who don't know me, my name is Wally Phillips and like you, I had money with the Cousins and like you, I got burned. I'd like to take a moment to introduce you to the other gentlemen at the table. On my far left is Frank Sommers, Frank is a reporter for the *Financial Digest* up in New York. We, our little group up here, felt it important to involve Frank because we want the people and especially the government up north to know of our situation. Frank is an old buddy. He knows all about Costa Rica Ex Pats and we can trust him." Wally could swear that he heard some oohs and ahs at Frank's introduction but continued, "Next, is Vito Russo, another victim. As many of you probably know, Vito is connected to some serious folks up in Brooklyn." As Wally said this, he put his finger to his nose and the crowd laughed. Wally continued with "Ok, now we have our old friend Marvin Greenbaum who knows a thing or two about accounting. Our last compadre is Dick Banks. Dick is retired from the Army where he did a lot of things we can't talk about if you get my drift."

The crowd murmured amongst themselves, many of them nodding to each other after Dick was introduced then broke into applause.

"Now, now, guys, hold it. We are no different than you. We have been victimized just like you and we thought it might be a good idea to form a group, appoint committees and try to do something about this mess."

A guy in the back hollered out. "Don't you think it's too late - I mean Ricky Hernandez already left the country with a good amount of our money?" Another shouted, "Yeah, what can we do about that?"

Wally, holding up his hands said, "Wait a second, we've got some ideas and we'd like to run them by you." More murmurs, then another guy yelled out, "Let him talk. Ain't none of us got any ideas at all." Another round of applause and Wally continued, "Look, no promises, but we feel that we should at least try by using our past experience from when we were up north making a living." Holding up a couple of clipboards he continued, "We'd like to know what expertise we have in this room. I'm gonna hand out these lists. One is for former cops or service men, one for lawyers, and one for accountants. We want to form committees, which will give us a three or four-pronged approach to this nightmare. Then we would have the committees all work together to decide our next course of action. Dick would head up the cops/soldiers committee, Marvin the accountants, and Vito and I the lawyers just to make sure of the legalities. I know it ain't much guys but it's a hell of a lot better than sitting on our butts and letting this happen," he said as he started handing out the clipboards.

Dick sat silently and thought that he must get a list of his people, go over resumes and interview them. He had the beginnings of a plan in his mind but wasn't ready to discuss it with the others. Not yet.

CHAPTER 15

———————— ■ ————————

JOURNEY'S END

After spending a week hiding out in various secluded mountain and jungle lodges all over Costa Rica, Ricky Hernandez, the fugitive cousin behind the now defunct investment scheme, was able to make contact with his former associates left over from the old Nicaraguan regime whom he had helped back in the turbulent eighties. For a price, they would help Ricky and his wife, Maria, hide out for however long they needed.

So it was arranged that they were picked up and then taken in their own muddy Ford Explorer for a late night drive by one of Somosa's ex bodyguards. After a grueling ride the car was carefully negotiating its way down a ravine. At the bottom, the driver announced that the 4-wheel drive could go no further in this swampy terrain. Ricky and his wife emerged from the back. Both were sleepy eyed and looked nervous. Ricky was clutching a black case.

They weren't really dressed for a hike through rough terrain, so they proceeded gingerly up the other side of the ravine. The driver was leading them with Maria bringing up the rear with occasional assistance from Ricky. Ricky was cursing the fact that his Italian loafers were getting ruined. At the top, they saw a breathtaking moonlit view of the largest lake in Central America, Lago De Nicaragua. The view they saw was deceiving. The lake was there all right but to get to it, they had to negotiate a treacherous swamp. They were about to cross into another country.

Just before dawn, they crossed near a Costa Rican village called *Mexico*, which put them in the swampy area just south of the lake. Finally, they stood on the small rise and down below, Ricky saw that there was a boat. Looking closer, the boat appeared to be some kind of military vehicle. In reality, it was a Grafton STAB (seal team assault boat) with twin Ford interceptor engines. The boat was manufactured for the U.S. Army back in 1969 and was used with some success in the Viet Nam conflict. After the war, the procommunist gorillas had purchased it from North Viet Nam to patrol the large lake and swamp area to prevent illegal arms shipments meant for the contras into Nicaragua. A man on the bow was waving to the Nicaraguan driver who turned to Ricky and said, "Senor, that man will take you to an island called Isla La Venada where the safe house is. Ricky took his wife's hand and carefully walked down the small hill to the boat.

What none of them could possibly have known was that a U.S. spy satellite jointly shared by the US CIA and DEA had been tracking their roundabout journey all the way from San José.

CHAPTER 16

---■---

AN IDEA

At the moment Ricky and his wife were stepping into the waiting boat, Dick Banks, along with Frank Sommers and Wally sat in Wally's apartment. They were in the process of going over resumes trying to make sense out of what kind of talent they had. Dick had not yet revealed his plan to the others but was about to let Frank in on some of it.

"See this guy, Donny Seneca?" Dick said.

"Yeah, I even met him once. Hangs out at the Gran Hotel Costa Rica Casino. He's a gambler and a nutcase. Always telling war stories and always paranoid about the Columbians that are after him," Wally told him.

"Well, I checked him out and he *was* an ops guy in the Columbian drug wars. He has had some success but suffered from a mental disorder brought on by the stress of always looking over his shoulder. They gave him an early retirement and put him out to pasture and he settled here because this was his safe haven between operations." Dick said.

"Yeah, well, he still looks unstable to me," Frank muttered.

"Frank, listen, the really good ones *are* a little wacko. If you understand them, they respond. I've had a lot of experience with this type. I could handle him. Met him a couple of times. He made me laugh," Dick said.

"Ok, what else you got," Frank asked.

"Slim pickings, too many old cops and ex GI's whose last action was WWII," Dick told him.

Then Frank blurted, "What are you putting together, anyway?"

Before answering, Dick stared at Frank for a long uncomfortable minuet. Then he took a swig of his beer and said, "This has gotta be off the record. Understood?"

Frank, a little reluctantly said, "Ok, off the record".

"Wally?"

"Sure, Dick, off the record," Wally said.

Dick took a deep breath and started, "Ok, I've got an idea and I don't want to tell the others for fear of getting them all worked up over something that might not even happen. Ok, here goes, I've got a buddy from my Special Ops days who is now DEA. He's been doing some checking for me and has access to the Canadian DEA who started this whole thing by ordering the raid in the first place. He also has access to satellite systems that can read your license plate from 100 miles up. He thinks he can locate Ricky's Explorer."

"What!" Frank said.

Dick continued, "Just hold on and hear me out. If and it's a big if, I can get a fix on where he is, I just might be able to form a team to perform an extraction and get him or the money back. That's why I'm interested in guys like Don Seneca. I could use at least one more as Ricky will probably have a good amount of security surrounding him. Ideally, I want to get to one of Ricky's guards so we can get intelligence but that's a tall order. But if all I get is two, I still think I can pull it off. One of the biggest problems I face is financing this thing because I'll need funds for weapons, equipment and payoffs. What I'm thinking is that after we get a go-ahead from our little group, we propose a very sketchy plan to the whole group and raise funds to pay for this scheme. They say he may have absconded with 450 million. We get half of that and it's more than enough to disburse amongst our little group of victims."

Before responding, Frank took a moment to compose his thoughts and said, "Ok, we've got about 100 guys. Let's say, for the sake of argument that 80% of them agree to finance the operation. How much you figure you'll need?"

"Ok, we need transportation, drivers, communication, and a plane with a pilot, bribe money, gear and weapons. A good educated guess would be about $50,000.00. Or about $500.00 a piece, if they all go for it," Dick said.

"Sounds low but you're the expert," Frank said.

"An operation like this doesn't cost much in terms of dollars but it can cost a lot in terms of lives. It's a dangerous proposition but knowing how these things go, I really don't see another alternative," Dick said.

"Should you pull it off, how's the best way to disburse the recovered money?" Frank asked.

"We should leave that to Marvin, our accountant but I would suggest that the guys who finance us make claim supported by documentation. Anything left over should be put into an interest bearing account so the others could make claim when the dust settles," Dick answered.

"Not a bad idea. We could handle it on a case by case basis *after* our investors are paid, but we're getting ahead of ourselves, aren't we?" Wally asked.

"You bet. If we decide to go ahead, I don't want to spell out the plan to anyone for fear of a leak. Ricky has ears all over town and I would need the element of surprise to pull this off," Dick said.

"Well, what's the next step then?" Frank asked.

"I'll start by getting a hold of my buddy in DEA. I've already given him the description of Ricky's SUV. Let's hope they were able to track him via satellite. Then, we let Marvin, Vito, and the others in on it. I have some recruiting to do. Then we raise money and then we pray," Dick's voice broke off at the word pray.

"Ok, I'll let the others know we need to meet. How about dinner tonight?"

As Dick got up to leave, he said "Yeah, dinner's fine. Right here. Wally cooks, right?"

Wally said something about take out from the KFC down the street.

Frank just smiled and walked Dick to the door saying, "I'll call the other guys and make it for eight."

CHAPTER 17

RECRUITMENT

As Dick got into the taxi, he told the driver to take him to the Gran Hotel Costa Rica. Inside, he was jubilant but you couldn't tell it from the grim look on his face. When he had gotten home, he had a message from Cummings. He hastily returned the call and Cummings told him the news: Ricky's Explorer had been located near a dock on the edge of Lake Nicaragua. From his early Special Ops exploits in that country, he knew there were some islands that would offer Ricky and his wife a secure hiding place. Hell, one even had a replica of a German Rhine Castle built on it. Now, in order to confirm which island Hernandez was holed up on, he needed the services of a money-hungry insider, which he was confident he would find.

He looked at his watch and saw that it was just about two o'clock. He had heard that Donny Seneca usually played rummy after lunch. Donny had a system where he would use the casino's courtesy chips and try to parley them into a small gain and then move on to the next casino and do the same. He would pick up a couple of thousand colones here and there but at the end, if his luck held, he'd wind up with 10 or 15 thousand colones. Not much but enough for dinner and a cheap hotel for the night not to mention a small stake for the next day's gambling. Donny lived from day to day.

As the cab pulled up to the hotel entrance, he paid the driver and noticed Wally's tico friend, Miguel hanging around trying to hustle some business form the Gringos exiting the hotel.

"Hola, Miguel, que paso?' Dick yelled as he approached.

"Hola, Señor Dick, come esta?" Miguel replied.

"Just trying to get by, amigo."

"You see Donny around?"

"Si, he's at the rummy table inside," Miguel answered.

"Gracias, Miguel. By the way, you still jumping out of perfectly good airplanes every weekend?" Dick joked.

"Si, but the wife doesn't like it much.' Miguel said.

Dick smiled as he said. "Don't hold me to it, but I might have something for you"

"Anytime Senor, anytime. You know where to find me," Miguel said as he waved Dick into the hotel.

As Dick entered the casino lobby he recalled that Miguel was a pretty good skydiver and that he just might have a pilot connection that could be useful. He also remembered that Miguel had a lot of contacts up in Nicaragua because he had done most of his jumping up there.

He spotted Donny doing his thing at the rummy table with all the pit bosses gathered around looking for Donny to cheat. Donny was just plain lucky and didn't need to cheat but his frequent runs of good luck always received suspicious stares from the pit bosses.

"Ola, Donny, come sta?" Dick said in Spanglish he came up to the table and took a seat to Donny's left.

"No Dick, not there, sit on my right. You'll screw up my cards!" Donny scolded.

Holding his hands up in surrender, Dick said, "Ok, ok, man. Not to worry," as he switched seats. In addition to being paranoid, Donny was very superstitious as most long time gamblers are. Donny was a relatively small man but he was wiry and possessed strength that sometimes even surprised him. He also had a facial twitch that dealers and other players found disconcerting. The twitch was a by-product of his rather illustrious military career.

As Donny won another hand, Dick put his hand on the table in front of Donny's chips and said, "Look, buddy, I need to talk to you and I don't have much time. How's about I buy you a late lunch?"

Donny looked at him strangely. Like many gamblers, he would rather play than eat and putting a hand between Donny and his chips could be dangerous for anyone but Dick. Finally, he said, "Anyone else, I'd cut their hand off, but since it's you, I'll let you buy me a drink but let's make it quick. I've got my rounds to make, you know."

Dick smiled and said, "It's a deal, come on." as he spun around on the stool and stood.

Donny meticulously gathered his chips, said thanks to the dealer and glared at the Pit Boss who just glared back and finally shook his head.

They went out to the plaza restaurant and took a table in the corner away from the other diners.

"Ok, Dick, what's so important that you have to drag me away from my game?"

"Fasten your seat belt, amigo. I take it you've heard about Ricky, one of the Cousins who just flew the coop?"

Donny shrugged and said "Sure, hasn't everyone? I mean, I read the papers like everyone else. Why? Did you have money invested with them?"

Dick smiled and said, "Didn't everyone?"

Donny shook his head and said "Just the minimum but to me that's a lot."

"Hundreds if not thousands of gringos had money tied up in it. Some guys had their life savings with them. Anyway, what I'm about to tell you is for your ears only. I can't stress that enough, Donny. As a matter of fact, let's make this conversation a hypothetical one, ok?" Dick said.

Donny twitched as he said, "Ok by me, amigo."

"Ok' Dick continued, "Suppose someone knew where Ricky was and had a way to get him and the money he took back to the investors? Would you be interested in being part of the hypothetical extraction team?"

Donny stared at him and almost screamed "What! You think you can pull it off? Are you nuts? He could be anywhere and I'm sure he's surrounded by body guards."

"Calm down man," Dick said as he looked around to make sure no one heard Donny's outburst. "Look, I just want to know if you still have it. Do you?"

"It's been a long time, Dick, I don't know. I've got this twitch. From time to time, I tend to overreact. Maybe but it depends on who else is involved," Donny answered.

"Right now, just you, me and maybe a tico skydiver. I'm also looking for an inside guy. I want a small force for what I'm thinking," Dick replied.

Donny thought and finally said with a small smile "Where?"

Dick knew that this was Donny's way of saying he'd do it, so he told him that he suspected Nicaragua but that he wasn't positive. Donny told him that he knew a couple of "Nicas" that might make for good guides or help find his inside guy. Dick told him to keep himself available. They stood, shook hands and Dick said that he would be in touch. Donny went back to the tables while Dick left for his next meeting.

Chapter 18

---■---

SETTLING IN

Although Hernández' found themselves in the lap of luxury, the island was also like a prison. Maria and Ricky were in the top floor Master Suite of the small castle built out of stone which rose straight up from the water. After the Second World War, a lot of Germans hastily relocated to various Central American countries including Nicaragua bringing with them their Aryan culture and, more importantly, money that allowed them to indulge in replicating Germanic Architecture. One example was this castle on the Isla La Venada in which Ricky and Maria now found themselves in exile. The castle was reminiscent of many of the famous castles built on small islands along the Rhine in Germany. They were almost storybook-like yet they were also virtual fortresses and very defensible against any invading army.

The master suite had been completely modernized and was very similar to a five star hotel suite one might find in Las Vegas. It had two levels with a spiral staircase that afforded breathtaking views of the lake and the shore beyond. It even sported a roman tub with a built-in Jacuzzi, wet bar, kitchen, and an oversized, round king bed.

Maria was bored and kept complaining. She missed her friends and the busy social life of San Jose and did not hesitate to tell Ricky.

"Enrique, why do we have to be here? I don't like it here. I want to go home," she whined as she filed her nails while lying in the big bed. She was clad in a sexy black lace negligee that should have attracted Ricky's attention but did not.

Ricky turned to her and yelled, "Maria, stop your bitching. The important thing is that we are safe here. Don't you realize that there are people in your precious San Jose that would turn you into the authorities as soon as look at you?"

Maria looked up and pouted using her voluptuous lips like a San Jose hooker, which she had indeed been. Ricky rolled his eyes and walked over to her with a small smile. He went to the closet and took out his briefcase, unlocked it and fiddled with the bottom, which was false. Under the false bottom was a jeweler's felt portfolio, which he removed. He opened the portfolio and showed Maria the diamonds he had been purchasing for the past five years. Some were as big as 10 or 15 carats, some were cut, some were polished some were set in earrings and rings. Ricky then told her what they were worth and she gasped.

"Maria, we live here another month, change our appearance then go to Europe, cash these in and live like royalty the rest of our lives. Be patient Mi Amor." With that, he kissed her passionately and Maria melted to his touch. They spent the rest of the afternoon making love, giggling like children and making plans for the big move.

---■---

CHAPTER 19

DINNER

N ow that Donny was lined up and his plan was coming together, he would have to contact Miguel about a pilot and a plane, Dick thought as he walked up Avenida Central towards the dinner meeting he had called with Marvin and Wally. He would have to tell them what he knew but he was reluctant because of Ricky's many ears in San Jose. The last thing he wanted was to lose the element of surprise but he also needed the money he thought as he entered the lobby elevator of Wally's building.

Knocking twice, he stood back as Frank opened the door and waved him in. Marvin and Wally were sitting on the couch. On the table, stood a couple of KFC buckets loaded with chicken. Marvin was munching on a leg. He started to rise as Dick said "No, no, Marv, stay there. Are you all right?" he said noticing that Marvin looked pale and shaky.

Wally interrupted and said, "He's a little worried about your calling a meeting without the others, Dick."

Looking a Marvin, Dick said, "Listen, the less the others know about this the better, for now. I want to fill you guys in. We're operating on a need to know basis."

"My God, a *need*-to- know basis," Marvin gasped, almost choking on his chicken.

"Look, everybody, relax. Let's take it one step at a time, ok? Wally, have you got a beer and some chicken for me?"

Wally went in the small kitchen while Dick took a seat opposite Marvin wondering why he was risking the health of an old man whose heart might not be able to take his talk of operations and cloak and dagger ways. As Wally gave him the beer and a leg, he smiled at both of them and started, "Ok guys, not to panic. I've been working on a plan to get some of the money back."

"How can you get *some* of the money? What is he talking about, Wally?" Marvin asked.

Wally just patted Marvin's knee and said, "Marvin, calm down, let him talk".

Marvin grimaced and nodded his head.

Dick said, "You all know my background. Without going into detail, I have contacts that can locate where Ricky is."

"YOU know where he is?' Marvin yelled as Wally and Frank just stared at him.

"I didn't say that. What I said is that I may have a plan to locate him, infiltrate his people, and get him and the money back to San Jose."

"What do you have to do in order to start on this plan?" Wally asked.

"Ok, good question, Wally. What I need you to do is call another meeting with the group. You, Marvin, Frank, and Vito head it up. You can tell them this: We *may* know where he went. We have a plan but we can't share it due to security reasons. We need money to implement the plan. We figure about $500.00 per investor. If they want a chance to get some of their money, it'll cost 'em. The whole operation hinges on your getting me financed."

"Can we tell them what the money's for?" Wally asked.

"No. Just tell them we have to keep it on a need-to-know basis."'

"Again with the need-to-know! Oye," Marvin uttered.

Dick smiled and said, "I've got a lot to do. You guys stay here, have dinner and discuss how you can sell this to the group. Without the money, we can't move forward."

"All right, but where are you going?" Frank's reporter mind asked.

"So sorry, no can tell. Let's just say I'm out recruiting." Dick said with a smile as he left.

CHAPTER 20

———————— ■ ————————

MORE RECRUITING

Dick found Donny grazing at the free buffet at the Colonial Casino on Avenida Primera. Donny never paid for food. He knew which casinos had free buffets for lunch or dinner, on which days, and he built his schedule around it. Dick suspected that without these free comp meals, Donny would never eat.

As Donny was piling chicken wings on his plate, Dick came up behind him and said, "Save some for the rest of us, buddy."

"Fuck you, you ugly bastard," Donny said with a smile.

With that, Dick grabbed some chicken and they found a quiet table upstairs in the sports book. Since there were no games on, they had the place to themselves.

Sitting down, Dick said "Tell me about these nicas you know. Do they need money?"

"You kidding, show me a nica who doesn't need money." Donny laughed. "They live in the underbelly here, but were well connected up north. Some kind of Para-military group, I think."

"Connected to the former regime?" Dick asked.

"Not sure but I think so."

Dick took a breath and said, "Don, I need someone inside to meet with them and try and find out anything they might know about their former employers who might be protecting Ricky and his wife out on an island in the middle of Lake Nicaragua."

"I understand, I'll give it a try."

"Try hard, amigo. Without an inside man to bribe, I don't have any other way. Call me the second you have something," Dick said as he rose to leave.

"Where the hell are you going?"

"Transportation arrangements, mi amigo," Dick replied as he turned to leave.

Once outside, he took a deep breath thinking the meeting with Donny had gone well. He smiled as he remembered that Don had told him his nicos lived on the underbelly side here in San Jose. He couldn't imagine any of Donny's acquaintances *not* living in that environment. One down, two to go he thought to himself as he turned west and started walking up Avenida Primera in the direction of the Gran Hotel. As he neared the circular driveway in front of the hotel's portico, he could see all the red taxis waiting in line. One extremely clean one stood out and he knew that Miguel would be in it.

Miguel was a little startled by the big gringo jumping into his passenger seat but took it in his stride saying, "We've got to stop meeting like this, senor. What will people think?"

Dick smiled and asked "How long of a wait for your fare?"

"Oh, maybe half an hour. Got anything to drink?"

"Stowe it, pal, you're on duty," Dick said as he pulled out a flask of his favorite tequila.

"Ok, you just go ahead and enjoy yourself, senor *una via*."

After taking a long slug, he handed the flask to Miguel and said, "Tell me about your pilot friend, amigo."

With that, Miguel took a slug and said, "That all? No problem. His name is Sanchez. Lives in San Pedro. Flys his Cessna out of a small airport out in the suburbs."

"How's business?" Dick asked.

"Like everyone, he struggles but pays the bills."

"Safe to say he needs money?'

"Damn right, don't we all?"

Dick smiled and said, "Ok, man, first off, this is confidential. It stays with you." Miguel nodded and Dick continued, "Find out if he's interested in a night run up to the Nicaraguan border with three, maybe four passengers taking a one way ride."

Miguel's eyes widened and he stared a Dick.

Undaunted, Dick continued, "Tell him it could happen in a week or two and I'll need to know how much. Got it?"

"Si, senor, but what's up?"

"I'll tell you more when I can. For now, just get the information and make sure your sky diving equipment is ready to go. Ok?" Dick said as he slipped the wide-eyed taxi driver a 10,000 Colone note.

As Dick got out of the taxi, Miguel started to ask another question but Dick just put his index finger to his mouth and said, "Mums the word. I'll check back tomorrow night." He closed the door and disappeared into the night crowd on the plaza.

One more stop, Dick thought as he bounded down Avenida Central in the direction of the Del Sol. Moments later, he strode into the crowed bar area and almost immediately, spotted his longtime favorite girlfriend, Juanita, and almost had to fight his way through the crowd to reach her. Girlfriend was really not the term he should be using for the relationship which had developed between them. She was more of a *favorita*, he thought.

She did her thing. He did his. She made good money in the prostitution game and it was legal. Every once in a while, Dick felt a jab inside but he was not about to tell anyone how to run their life. He was comfortable with the way things were, and he saw no reason to change the situation.

After finally reaching her, they hugged for a moment and he said, "What a crowd. You busy?"

"Never too busy for you, mi amor," she said as her hand slid down to his crotch area.

Laughing, he said "Oooh, that feels good, mi amor, but not now, I just want to talk."

Pouting that famous San Jose hooker pout, she moaned, "Oooo, mi amor, I really want you tonight. Talk? Ok, but you owe me. I know you want me. Maybe later?"

"Of course, mi amor, at my house, later, but for now, let's just go somewhere quiet where we can talk," he said as he took her hand and led her in the direction of the coffee shop.

They took a corner table in the back. Once they ordered coffee and the waiter had gone Juanita said, "Mi amor, I've got a couple of rich gringos waiting, can you make this conversation *muy rapido*?"

Dick took a 10,000 Colone note out his pocket, slid it over to her and said with a smile, "Not to worry, mi amor, it won't take long and you might make more than that if you can help me."

"*Muy bueno mi amor*," she said with a small smile.

"Juanita, I may need your help in convincing a young nica to give you some information. I'll need you to use your feminine powers to get this guy to tell you something about what his employers are up to."

"Dick, is this dangerous for me?"

"It would be for me, but not for you. It will involve some overnight travel to Nicaragua."

"That, mi amor, will cost more."

"Comprende, mi amor," Dick said.

"When?" she asked becoming more businesslike.

"Maybe as soon as a couple of weeks. I can't give you the exact time, but I'll contact you. Try to keep your social calendar open."

"*Por Usted, Yo lo hare, mi Amor.* (For you, I will, my love) But now, I've got to make money. *Permitame*," (excuse me) she said as she got up.

"Of course," Dick said as he rose and kissed her on the cheek. She hurried back to the bar and he took a moment to finish his coffee and reflect. He was pleased with the results of the last couple of hours. He had Donny, Miguel and Juanita all working for him. Tomorrow would prove interesting.

Frank, who had spotted him from the entrance, interrupted his thoughts.

"Where the hell have you been?" Frank asked.

"Evening Frank, I've been working."

Frank, with a frown, sat down across from Dick and said, "I'd like to be working but I don't have a thing to write. You promised me an exclusive and I'm wondering if you're leaving me out of the loop."

"Frank! How can you say such a thing? We just had a meeting at Wally's. Right?"

"Yeah, but I think you've got more juicy stuff. What are you up to anyway?"

"Damn it Frank, you're a reporter and I'm putting a precise operation together. Do you expect me to give you all the details before I can implement my plan? If this were 1944, would you expect me to reveal the invasion plans for D Day?"

At this, Frank flushed and said, "I don't want to compromise anything. Can't you just throw me a bone now and then? You know I won't print anything without your permission."

Dick let out a breath and said, "Ok, here's a bone. I've been recruiting."

"Damn it, Dick, you told me that when you left Wally's," Frank interrupted.

This drew a smile from Dick who said, "Can't trick you, can I?" Ok, I trust you but keep this under your hat. I know where he's hiding, I know how to find out where the money is, and I know how to get in and out. I hope to do it soon. That enough?"

"How soon?" Frank shot back.

"That depends on our partners getting me the money. Operations like this can cost a pretty penny. How did things go after I left?"

"Marvin, Wally and Vito did a lot of phone work. Seems they created some kind of telephone tree after our last meeting. Everyone's set to meet at ten tomorrow morning at the upstairs sports book of the Colonial."

Dick's eyebrows rose up as he said, "Wow, that's better than I had hoped for."

As Dick rose, Frank said, "Where you going?"

Throwing money on the table, Dick said, "Even military genius' have to sleep."

CHAPTER 21

THE FINAL MEETING

T hey all had come. The official count was 97. Some were skeptical, some hopeful, but all were ready to hear what their new leaders had to say. The seating was limited so some had to line up along the walls. Once everyone was seated, the ex-cops took up positions by the doors to insure security. Wally banged a glass on the table and the mild roar quickly ceased. "Ok, guys, we've been working on the situation and we have some ideas. Now it's time for you to listen and make decisions." He couldn't help noticing that all eyes looking at him became questioning, but he continued, "Yes, you," he pointed to one in the back, then to another and said, "you and you," pointing to yet another.

"First off, I have a hypothetical question. If I were to tell you that I knew the whereabouts of one Senor Enrique Hernandez and had a way to recover your investment, would you be willing to pay me $500.00 each to get your money back?"

A wave, a shock seemed to take over the room. As he looked around, all Wally could see were blank looks with mouths agape. As it sunk in, hands went up, and Wally began fielding questions many of which he couldn't answer.

One guy wanted to know exactly where Ricky was. "Can't answer that," Wally replied.

Another asked, "How do you know?"

"Can't tell you that either," Wally answered.

Another said, "What you're saying is that you can get us our money but need money from us to do that.'

"Exactly," Wally said.

"How do we know we can trust you?" Another shouted from the rear.

"You don't. But understand that the committees you approved have been working non-stop on this for the past few weeks and it is our combined opinion that this can be done but it needs financing. Without that financing, it's not possible. Gentlemen, it's your decision. Marvin, Vito and I will now leave the room. You've got 15 minutes to decide. If you agree, you'll be in your seat when we get back, if you don't, you can leave and none of us will think any the less of you. But remember, any monies recovered will be used to pay those who provided financing for the operation. What's left will go into a trust and you can fight with the lawyers for your split. Remember, the four of us were investors too. With that, he pulled $500.00 out of his wallet, threw it down on the table, looked at Marvin and Vito and said, "Let's go, guys." With that, they too rose and threw down their 500.00. Then all three left the room.

Out in the anteroom, Frank said "Wow, that was a gutsy move!"

"I just hope it works." Wally said as he lit a cigarette. Marvin was rubbing his head. Vito looked worried but said nothing. "Wish Dick had been here" Wally said.

"He's out setting the whole thing up. This part of the deal belongs to you guys." Frank said.

"Yeah, guess so. How long has it been?" Wally asked.

"Bout ten minutes and I haven't seen anyone leave,." Vito said.

Just then, the door burst open and seven or eight red-faced guys went out. With that, Wally said, "It's time, guys, let's go."

As they strode into the room, Wally was pleased to note that about ninety souls had remained. He couldn't help but grin as he said, "Hope you've all got your checkbooks, because the sooner we get financed, the sooner we'll get our money back."

"Not so fast, Wally," a man in the middle said as he stood. Wally recognized him as a retired accountant he knew from the poker tables.

"Hey Jim, what's up? Er, I mean the chair recognizes Jim Marsh."

Marsh said, "Thank you. My name is Jim Marsh and I've been elected as the spokesman for the group that remained. We want you to know that we've agreed to providing the operation with $500.00 apiece but we will expect a full accounting of how the money is spent and we would like a refund of any unused funds should there be any when the operation is over. We also would like a written contract signed by the four of you stating you have received the monies and what the intended use is."

"Sounds like a legal mind at work,' Wally replied and turned with a smile to Marvin and asked, "Any problem with Mr. Marsh's proposal, Marvin?"

Marvin said no as he pulled open his laptop and added that he would have the contract ready in a few minutes.

Wally smiled and said, 'Ok by my count, there's ninety in favor plus the four or us which makes ninety four which equals forty seven thousand dollars. I make a motion that we accept the aforementioned funds in order to provide financing for an operation to recover investments made by the group with the Cousins. Do I have a second?"

His smile grew as he heard almost a hundred seconds ring out from the crowd.

CHAPTER 22

A PLAN COMES
TOGEATER

Dick was sleeping but the persistent ringing of the phone finally woke him. As he reached for the phone, he noticed the clock said it was 6:00 AM. Juanita, sleeping next to him, barely stirred. "This better be good", he mumbled into the phone.

Wally's strong morning voice boomed, "You bet its good, sleepyhead. We got the money!"

"How much?"

"Forty-seven thousand plus your five hundred to make it forty-seven thousand, five hundred," Wally told him.

"Hmmm, that'll work, but I'll have to be a smart shopper," Dick said into the phone.

"Ok, what's the next step?" Wally asked.

"Good question. First off, I need to meet with Donny and Miguel to get their updated reports. I'll give you guys a call after that. Ok?"

Wally said ok, and they hung up. He gave Juanita a slap on the butt as he got out of bed. She moaned and buried herself further in the sheets.

After making some strong coffee, taking a shower, and sitting down at his small desk, Dick once again reached for the phone and dialed Donny's number. He answered on the second ring and with some authority, which surprised Dick, as Donny was never known as a morning person.

"Buenos Dias, amigo, it's Dick"

"Right back at ya, compadre," Donny shot back.

"Got anything for me?"

Donny took a deep breath and started, "I got a hold of my nica last night and he called back this morning. Actually, I was just getting ready to call you when the phone rang. Anyway, one of them has a cousin who shows up in Rivas, that's a town on the lake known for its fishing industry."

"Skip the tour, just tell me where it is and why it's important to us." Dick snapped.

"Maybe you should switch to decaf, amigo," Donny quipped but continued, "Ok, it's about an hour north of the Costa Rican border and this kid, you know, the cousin of my guy? Well, anyway, he's got a new gig. He's a security guard out on a small island with a huge castle built into the volcanic rock. My guy says that one of the kid's duties is to come into Rivas every few days on a launch where he helps load up supplies. My guy says the kid is nice, but not that bright. Name's Julio."

Dick asked, "How's he fixed for money?"

"A lot better than he was a few weeks ago. Jobs are scarce north of Costa Rica."

"You think he might have a weakness for the ladies?" Dick asked.

"For God's sake, he's nineteen and now he's got a little money in his pocket. What do you think?"

"I think I've got a call to make. Call me tonight," Dick said as he hung up.

Dick made a call to Miguel, gave him instructions to alert the pilot to be ready for a night flight within the next two weeks. He also made arrangements for Miguel to pick him and Juanita up the next morning. As he and Juanita got ready for bed, he couldn't help thinking that this may actually work.

CHAPTER 23

---■---

A BUS RIDE TO NICARAGUA

Juanita and Dick rode in the back of Miguel's taxi to the "Coca Cola" bus terminal, which was where the big buses left for Nicaragua. Juanita listened quietly as Dick explained about the young guard and his schedule. At one point, she interrupted to ask what he looked like and how she would recognize him. Dick answered by telling her that he was a good looking young nica, and he'd be the driver of the boat and he would be alone for the two hours or so it took for his compadre to shop for supplies in town.

"At least tell me his name, mi amor," she scolded.

Dick looked at her and said "Sorry mi amor, its Julio and he wears a brown kaki uniform. I should have told you that first."

"Si, mi amor, it would help. Now, tell me exactly what information you would like me to get from this young hombre."

"Ok, good. First I need confirmation that there is an important couple from Costa Rica staying on an island and which island. We think it's Isla de Venado. We think there's a castle on that island. Then I need to know where in the castle the important guests are staying plus how many guards or bodyguards there are and their locations around the island."

"Anything else, mi amor", she said with a hint of sarcasm.

Dick smiled and took her hand and kissed it as he said, "If anybody can pull this off, it's you, mi amor. Remember, he's young, good looking and there are no women out on that island. He's gotta be horny as hell."

Juanita took the compliment with a smile and looked out the taxi window to see that they were pulling up in front of the small terminal where people were lined up to board their buses.

Before they got out, Dick handed her round trip tickets and a hundred thousand colones (about $200.00) and said, "That's half, you get the other half when you come back with information. Call me as soon as you get in.

I'll pick you up here. Bueno?"

"Si mi amor, Juanita always gets her man." With that, she blew him a kiss and got out and went over to her line. She only had to wait fifteen minutes or so before she boarded the big luxury bus. Once she found her seat, she sat down and settled in for the eight-hour journey north.

While the scenery was nice, Juanita chose to sleep but had trouble because of the many potholes. It was almost as if the driver went out of his way to hit every single one. Her thoughts drifted to Dick. Didn't he realize that she would have done this for nothing? She had fallen for him but she had no idea where the relationship would lead. It was her dream that some nice gringo would eventually take her away from the life she had chosen for herself. The money, of course was good. She probably earned more than most bank presidents in Costa Rica. But there were some pretty bad aspects about her life that worried her. The danger, for instance. She had been beaten, stabbed and robbed while plying her chosen trade. She wanted out but wasn't positive if Dick was her Knight in shining armor. Maybe, she thought as she finally started to drift off.

At the border, some six hours later, everyone got off the bus for the required immigration check. She patiently stood in line with everyone else. Long lines that take hours are common in Central America and it did no good to be impatient. Finally, she arrived at the spot where two armed guards stood behind an immigration officer who looked very official and serious. He checked her passport and asked the purpose of her visit. She said she had friends to visit in Rivas. He gave her the once over and his eyebrows went up when he realized how attractive this tica was. His gaze rested on her ample breasts as he stamped her documents and handed them back with a smile, which she readily returned.

As she re-boarded the bus for Rivas, she glanced at her watch knowing she had about an hour to spare once she arrived in the small fishing village. The bus made good time and an hour later, she disembarked at a small soda (snack bar) which was in site of the docks where the boats came in. Hungry, she sat down in the soda for a quick rice and chicken meal, which she washed down with a "té frio" or iced tea.

She arrived at the dock with about a half hour to spare. She looked about and saw that there were plenty of empty berths as most of the fishing boats were out on the vast lake. She looked to the East and noticed several volcanic islands rising out of the calm waters. As she was wondering which island might be the one where one of the notorious Cousins was in exile, she picked up the wake of a small military looking vessel heading straight towards the docks. As it grew closer, she saw that it was an olive drab color and its shape reminded her of a pleasure trawler she had seen on one of her many visits to the beaches of Costa Rica. She could make out two khaki clad men in the cockpit as it reached the inner buoys and had to slow down a bit.

The berth for this boat was practically right in front of her, along the seawall, just beneath her. Once the boat docked, the two men, one older and one younger spoke for a while, the older one seemed to be giving instructions and then he got up on the seawall, waved goodbye to his associate, saying something like h*asta* (later) and walked off in the direction of town.

Juanita could see that the young man that remained was keeping busy with paperwork and charts. He was in deep concentration which gave her a chance to slip undetected down to the dock. Next, she stood in front of the gangway in full view of the young nica who glanced up and saw before him a beautiful young girl dressed in tight jeans and a belly button shirt. He smiled and said something like "What are you doing here, Mami?" She smiled back and asked if he had something cold to drink as she waved at her face as if to indicate she was roasting in the hot sun.

He came out of the small cockpit and extended his hand inviting her to get out of the hot sun. She smiled up at him as she grabbed his hand. Once in the shade, he bent over a cooler and offered her a beer. She thankfully accepted. He grabbed one too and they toasted each other and both took a long gulp. She looked up at him with grateful eyes and smiled again and said,

"Mi nombre es Juanita, Cómo se llama usted?" He answered Julio and she told him that was her father's name.

Each sip of beer brought another smile and another step closer to Julio who was visibly overwhelmed by this beauty who had so unexpectedly come into his life. Before he knew it, she was at his side rubbing the chest hairs beneath his shirt. Julio was starting to breath hard and Juanita knew it was time to get a little information before she proceeded further.

"Julio, you have a very nice boat here. You must be a very important man."

He smiled and said, "No, Juanita, I am simply the driver of this boat that belongs to my employer."

"You must work for a very important man, then." She stated.

"Si, Juanita, he lives out on a big island in the lake. It's called Isla de Venada"

"Ohh, he must be very rich," she said as her hand undid another button on his shirt.

"Si, este hombre es muy rico." He said as his face flushed.

"Mmmm, mi amor," she said as her hands went further south.

Just as she started to toy with the waistband on his pants, she asked if that was the island where the very rich hombre from Costa Rica was living. This gave him pause and he asked how she knew about that. Playing with his trouser button, she told him that she was from Costa Rica and everyone there knew about this famous man. She also told him that everyone in Costa Rica loved and admired this man. This seemed to assuage his concerns and at this point she found the zipper and smiled up at his beet red face as she started lowering it.

About halfway down, she felt his hardness and said, "Oooo, mi amor" as she looked lovingly into his eyes. He looked a little embarrassed but happy and she gave him another smile as her hand reached inside to caress his manhood. Julio gave out a sigh and took a deep breath.

Time for another question Juanita thought and lunged forward in her husky bedroom voice, "Julio, mi amor, does my countryman travel with his wife, Maria?"

Startled, he said, "You know Señora Maria?"

"Si, mi amor, she is also very well-liked by all Costa Rican women. She is very famous!" Juanita said as she stroked his groin area.

"Ohhhh, Juanita," he replied.

Juanita repositioned herself in front of him, reached up and pulled his pants all the way down to his knees. When she saw his huge erection, she complimented him on his organ, which she knew from experience, impressed men a lot. Just as she moved in with her darting tongue, she asked one more question, "Mi amor, this couple, where do they stay on your island?"

Without even thinking or being suspicious, he said, "Oh, they stay on the top floor Master Suite which is reserved for visiting dignitaries."

With that, Juanita moved in on the throbbing member as if it were a cool Popsicle on a hot day, which was ok with Julio who was having the time of his life. Later, in the afterglow and before she made a graceful exit, she asked about bodyguards and was told there were several, one just outside the suite, two at the entrance, and three (including himself) patrolling the grounds.

At this point, she decided that this guy was so sex hungry that she could get more. Like long acquainted lovers, she talked to him about coming to visit her in San Jose and being naive, he took the bait and had visions of shacking up with Juanita in her luxurious City apartment. Then she sweetened the pot by slipping him enough money for bus fare saying that he should come down as soon as he could get away. What he said next almost floored her but being the good actress she was, she contained herself.

As she was preparing to leave, he told her that he'd be there sooner than later as his job would be coming to an end soon because the rich couple would be leaving not long after the skin doctor came.

"Skin Doctor?" Juanita asked.

"Si mi amor, there is a doctor that my boss is sending for. He's a gringo and his specialty is changing the face so your own mother don't know you," he said with a knowing smile.

Juanita, knowing this was important information pressed forward. "So, when is this Gringo Doctor coming, mi amor?"

"He come in two weeks and then they leave so I come see you, No?"

"Por supuesto, mi amor (of course)," she said as she scribbled out her phone number and told him to call tomorrow and she would make plans for him to stay with her. Then, she reached up and gave him a deep passionate kiss like he never had received in his life. With that, she backed off the boat, waved good-by numerous times and climbed up on the seawall and turned toward the town and the bus station. Wow, Senor Dick will like this she thought.

CHAPTER 24

———————————————■———————————————

A CHANGE IN PLAN

"Wait! What did you say? A plastic surgeon is coming to the island in two weeks and they'll leave shortly after!" Dick's yelling was scaring Juanita, not to mention Miguel who sat in the front seat of the cab as they both listened to Juanita's report.

"Don't get mad at me, Dick, I just get the information you asked for but he tell me more," she yelled back.

"No, no, no, Mi Amor, I'm not mad at you. I am very happy. You did a great job and I love you for it. I'm just a little surprised. Now, you're sure this Julio knows what he speaks of?"

"Si, he's just telling me what all the other guards know. No reason for him to lie to me."

"Ok, here's the rest of the money, you really earned it. Take another taxi, go home, clean up and rest. I'll be there as soon as I can."

"Gracias, mi amor," she said as she got out of the cab. Then she turned back, leaned into the passenger side of the taxi and said, "One more thing, mi amor, young Julio will be calling me in the next day or so to arrange another rendezvous here in San Jose."

Dick thought that this could work to their advantage. He took her hand and kissed it with a smile and said, "You did a terrific job mi amor. Good thing, I'm not the jealous type."

"Where to, amigo?" Miguel said as he pulled out of the bus terminal.

"Let's go find Donny."

"That would be the Casino Radisson. They serve free buffet everyday about this time." Miguel chuckled as he slipped it into second.

Dick sat in the back thinking. He now had a deadline and had to move forward quickly. He was delighted that Juanita might have found him the perfect inside man. He couldn't get the Doctor thing out of his mind. If Ricky changes his appearance and flees to Europe, he could blend in and spend the rest of his life free from the worry of being captured. Ricky was one smart bird. He'd have to be smarter he thought as Miguel pulled up in front of the Raddison Casino entrance.

Dick looked up and said, "You go get him, Miguel. I'll wait here. When you bring him back, we'll all take a ride to the park."

Before Dick could finish a smoke, Miguel was back with Donny in tow. They all piled into the cab and headed for nearby Park Morazan where they could talk in private, face to face. Once they found a secluded bench Dick updated Donny with the information Juanita had brought back.

"Is she one hundred percent sure?" Donny asked.

"Yes and so am I," Dick replied.

"Hmmm, this really puts a damper on your plans, huh?"

"Yes and no. It may be a blessing in disguise. If we could find out who this Doctor is, maybe we could replace him with our own. That way, we'll have an advance man inside the castle."

Donny let out a breath and asked how they could find out who the Doctor is and what he looked like.

Dick looked Donny squarely in the eye and said, "If he looks like a gringo, one of us might be the perfect candidate."

Donny just stood looking at Dick with a blank look but after a couple of seconds, the light went on in his eyes and he said, "Are you nuts? Are you suggesting that one of us impersonate this guy and try to fool Enrique, his protectors and all those body guards?"

"Yes, Donny that's exactly what I'm suggesting"

Donny, a bit exasperated said, "Look, even if one of us could pawn ourselves off as a Doctor, we still don't know who he is or what he looks like not to mention if he is in Nicaragua or if there flying him in from the States."

Dick snapped his finger loud enough that both Donny and Miguel jumped and said, "Wait a minute, Juanita told me that the kid will be calling tomorrow! If I can get a name, I can track him down with the help of my former employer's Intel computer programs. Then, at least, we'll have a picture. I have to call Juanita right now."

With that, Miguel handed Dick his cell phone and Dick dialed the number. He quickly told Juanita that she needed to get the good doctor's name and get back to him as soon as possible.

Handing the cell back, he said to Miguel, "That pilot ready to go?"

"Si amigo. He's on standby, but he wants a deposit. Half the money."

"No problem, I'll stop by Wally's place and get money. I'll also need it for some weapons. Donny, you got that all arranged, right?"

Donny looked hurt and said, "Hey, man, you asked me to set it up. I set it up. The nicas have the automatics with silencers, smoke and stun grenades and the parachutes you asked for. All you gotta do is fork over like 12 grand in gringo dinero."

"Sorry to be so jumpy, Don, I'm just a little stunned by the recent turn of events. My head is spinning, but it's all coming together. Ok, Miguel, can you take Don and me to Wally's? We need to get this show on the road."

"I hope this Doctor doesn't shave his head," Donny said as they got in.

CHAPTER 25

———————— ■ ————————

THE DOC

Once they got to Wally's apartment, Dick counted out twelve thousand and gave it to Donny telling him it was for the weapons and to go straight to the nicas with it and no stopping off at any casinos that might be on the way. Donny, looking hurt sheepishly smiled and took the money and left. Then he counted out five more representing the deposit for the pilot. He gave it to Miguel and told him to tell the pilot he gets the other half when we're over the drop zone. Miguel nodded and also left. That leaves thirty something grand. I hope like hell I'm not squandering the needed bribe and payroll money, Dick thought. Exhausted, Dick almost collapsed on Wally's couch.

"You look like hell, Dick, when are you going to rest?" Wally said.

"Can't, I've got more calls to make."

Wally asked if he wanted to use his phone but he declined saying that his phone at home was secure, plus he had all the numbers there.

After thanking Wally profusely for all the effort he made getting the money, Dick left and caught a cab home.

As soon as he got home, he looked up the number for Cummings at CIA and placed a call. He had to leave a message. He hung up the phone and leaned back on the sofa and was asleep in 2 minutes.

While Dick slept, a certain Dr. Eric Golightly was explaining the basics of a nose job to a snobby teenager in his lavish Beverly Hills office on Wilshire Boulevard. While she asked yet another stupid question, his nurse would field, he thought about Las Vegas and his favorite game, Texas Hold 'Em. The good Doctor was an addict when it came to poker. He played in LA, Vegas, Reno and anyplace there was a game. His wildly successful Beverly Hills practice paid for most of it in the beginning but he had been on losing streak for the past few months. Nothing serious, he told himself he'd come out of it. He just needed some cards to come his way. They didn't, and suddenly, he found himself deep in the hole and he could no longer keep going to the trough at the practice without his partners becoming suspicious. He already had taken some out using some phony patient records but it was just a matter of time before they uncovered his embezzlement.

Then he thought back on the visit he received last week: A couple of seedy looking guys from some Central American country, Nicaragua maybe, he couldn't quite remember. Anyway, they had known about his problem and had offered him a way out. Go down there to Nicaragua or whatever banana republic it was and perform some quick plastic surgery on some spic's face. God, what a mess, he thought. I don't even speak Spanish and I hate the thought of going to some third world country but I have to because the partners are getting suspicious. He had to replace that money and quickly, he thought. Oh, well, it'll be a quick in and out. No major job, just a nip and tuck type of thing to change this guy's facial appearance. If all went well, he could be back in LA in two or three days. He felt once again in his lab coat pocket for the ticket that they gave him. First class to Managua, Nicaragua on the 15th of the month. He was to be met by 3 security guys representing a Senor Hernandez. Just under two weeks from today, he thought as he looked at the wall calendar.

As the good Doctor was looking at his calendar in California, Dick was suddenly awakened from his nap in Costa Rica by the rude sound of his ringing phone.

"Banks", he shouted into the phone.

"Hola, mi amor, why you sound so mad?" Juanita said.

"Sorry Juanita, I was sleeping and forgot where I was for a moment."

"No hay problema, Señor Dick. I just call to tell you that my horny nica called already and he let it slip that when he returned to the island, they told him that he will be going to the Managua Aero Puerto to pick up a Doctor Eric Golightly from Los Angeles, California on the 15th."

"Juanita, you're a gem. That was quick."

"Remember, Juanita always gets her man. He can't wait to come see me. He thinks I live in the lap of luxury here in San Jose."

"Well, thanks for getting back so soon. It's a big help," he said his goodbyes and hung up. Great! Now he had a name. He got up, went to the kitchen to make a cup of coffee. As he was walking back to the living room, coffee in hand, the phone rang again.

"Hello?" Dick spoke into the phone

"Banks, you lucky son of a bitch. Living the good life in Costa Rica," Cummings teased.

"Ah, you could call it that. Guess what, I need another favor".

"Natch, why else would you call?"

"Yeah, I can be a pain. Anyway, there's this American doctor that will be flying from Los Angeles to Managua on the 15th."

"And?" Cummings said.

Dick took a breath and said "And I need him intercepted and detained for at least 72 hours."

"Dick, you're asking a lot. In the old days, maybe, but now it's tough. This place is run by congress and the administration. Bunch of party poopers. All they talk about is what's politically correct."

"Come on, Cummings, I really need some help here."

Cummings sighed and said, "I said *we* couldn't do it, I never said anything about our counterparts in Nicaragua not doing it."

"You're kidding! You can do that? I'll owe you big, Cummings."

"Don't worry, soldier you'll pay big time. You got a name for me or do I have to do all the work?"

"The name is Dr. Eric Golightly and his office is in Beverly Hills. He's set to fly on the 15th out of LAX to Managua. Sorry, I don't know the flight or airline."

Cummings laughed and said he thought he might be able to determine that, but in the meantime, he'd run a computer check and get back to Dick as soon as he had the information.

"Ah, one more thing?"

"And what would that be trooper?"

"I'll need a picture of him."

"You got a fax, you got a picture."

"I really appreciate this Cummings," Dick said into the phone.

All that Cummings said in reply was "*forgetaboutit*" and the line went dead.

CHAPTER 26

———————— ■ ————————

THE OPS PLAN

A week later the five men key to the operation and Juanita were sitting in Wally's apartment listening to Dick explain that the doctor would be arriving in Managua at 2:00 pm one week from today off Taca flight 276 from LA. Dick looked into their faces as he told them. Donny sat on the couch next to Miguel and Juanita. Frank sat in Wally's favorite armchair and one of Donny's nicas, a trained killer, sat backwards on one of Wally's kitchen chairs listening intently as Donny translated Dick's words into Spanish. Dick then asked Frank to get the lights as he turned on a slide projector and the image of a good looking blonde haired man dressed in a lab coat filled Wally's dining room wall.

"Whew, Man, he looks like you, Dick!" Donny shouted halfway out of his sofa seat.

"Well, that settles it. I guess I'm the Doc. Juanita tells me that with a little make up and a haircut, both administered by her, I should be able to pull it off. Too bad he wasn't a bald guy, eh Don?" Dick said as he gave Donny a wink.

Frank, mouth agape asked what in hell was going on.

"Easy Frank, it's about to become crystal clear. By the way, you told me you used to skydive. Is that still the case?"

"Well, it's been about a year but I try to keep up. What's that got to do with this?" Then, thinking, his eyes bulged and he started to say something but not much came out.

"Calm down, Frank. I haven't even got to the good part," Dick said with a smile. "Ok, guys and girls, I've kept you in suspense long enough. What I propose is this, Six days from today, I'm flying up to the Managua airport. Meanwhile, arriving on a flight from the states will be the doctor you see here. By the way, his specialty is plastic surgery and he's been hired to alter Senor Enrique Hernandez' face so that he can flee undetected to his next and final hiding place probably somewhere in Eastern Europe. The good doctor, however, will never make it to the Managua baggage claim area. He will be taken into custody and held by Nicaraguan Secret Police who don't speak a lick of English."

"Let me guess," Frank said. "You're going to replace him!"

"Bingo Frank! No more interruptions, ok? Ok, Frank's right, my plan is to walk into the waiting arms of Enrique's henchman at the airport. Everyone tells me that because of Juanita's handiwork I'll be a dead ringer for the Doc. Let's hope so because these guys have no sense of humor. Ok, next I pile into the car with them for the two-hour trip to Rivas and then the one hour boat ride to the island fortress. Oh, didn't I mention that we found Enrique sitting pretty on an island in Lake Nicaragua protected by elements of the former Nicaraguan Regime? Well, now you know."

Frank sat dumbfounded in the chair shaking his head back and forth.

Donny, Miguel and Juanita just smiled since they already knew much of what Frank was hearing for the first time.

"With me, I'll have my little medical bag which will contain all the normal Doctor stuff plus a prepared syringe of what is commonly known as truth serum plus another to knock out his wife out for a long time. The only operating I'll be doing on Enrique is giving him a shot so that he can tell me where the diamonds are hidden."

"Diamonds!" Frank shouted and half rose out of his chair spilling his coke.

"Yes, diamonds Frank, how else would you transport over four hundred and fifty million bucks? As you know, I have friends in CIA, DEA and FBI. They tracked Enrique's banking and buying habits going back the last five years. Ok, Frank? Now, if there are no further interruptions," Dick said as he clicked the slide projector to reveal a bird's eye view of the island fortress.

"What you're looking at in this shot is the castle fortress built some forty years ago by rich German ex-pats on the Isle La Venada in the middle of Lake Nicaragua."

Depicted on the wall, there were three shots: one showing the entire volcanic island, one showing the part of the island's windward side where the faux Rhine Castle was surrounded by lake water on three sides and the last was a satellite shot looking straight down into the courtyard. Dick gave them a moment to absorb the pictures and then said, "Ok, the courtyard is approximately 50 meters square, that's about 500 square feet and it will be your drop zone, Donny. You'll be jumping at night. Think you can do it?"

"Piece of cake for me and Carlos, but I may have to train our friend Frank." Frank jumped up shouting, "You're not serious. No one in their right mind would even consider that jump in daylight much less at night."

Dick smiled and said, "No one ever said Donny was in his right mind. But, if anyone can do it, Donny can and he would do it blindfolded if I let him. I do have some good news for you though. I looked it up and they'll be a full moon that night."

Donny loved it and smiled as he said to Frank, "I'll have you doing it your sleep, Frank, just give me three days. Don't worry. Look, the nica's not worried."

"Damn it, Donny, he doesn't speak enough English to understand what the hell we're talking about!" Frank shot back.

With that, the Nica got up, walked over to Frank, flipped his lapel back to reveal his US Army jump wings, smiled at him and said, "Hoorah, Mother Fucker". He then calmly walked back to his spot on the sofa. Frank just gaped and sat back down in his chair.

"Ok, looks like you three will be my rescue party. Try not to disturb any guards till we hook up. Juanita's new boyfriend will meet you in the courtyard at 1:00am. He'll bring you to me. By then, I hope to have the diamonds in my possession."

"What's our exit strategy?" Donny asked.

"That's where Juanita comes in. Juanita, how goes the romance?'

Juanita smiled and said, "He's coming down tomorrow on the bus. He is dreaming of spending the weekend with his new love. I may save you some money. He will do anything for me, Dick."

"Only if you're 100% sure, I need him to drive that boat for us. There's no other way off that island for us. Don't take a chance. I'll have the money ready."

"No problema, mi amor," she said sheepishly.

"Ok, now that we know how we're getting off, how we getting in, Miguel?"

Miguel responded quickly. "Pilot knows the date. Jumping gear is ready. Long range forecast calls for a clear, moonlit night. I also took care of your papers, Dick. It's amazing how easy and cheap it is to duplicate a phony passport."

"Good work, Miguel. Donny?"

"Weapons and tactical equipment are ready to be picked up from the storage area and loaded into the SUV Miguel is getting for us. All I have left to do is train Frankie boy here," Donny said as he nodded towards Frank.

"Ok, now Frank, you know why you're part of this?"

"No, not really."

"We want you to know exactly what happened so you can document what went down in an orderly fashion. We need accuracy as we're going to have to account for a lot of money. Since there are international borders involved, we might need documented proof of what went down. It's also payback. We owe you for sitting on the story so long."

"Thanks, I'm running out of excuses for my editor," Frank said.

Dick nodded and told everyone to go about his or her business for the rest of the week. They should go to work, don't talk about it to anyone and check in with him by phone daily. He also told them that Miguel would take him to the airport. He would give them any final instructions once Dick was enroute.

CHAPTER 27

JUMP TRANING

Since Frank had previous experience from his skydiving club, Donny first had to find out what Frank didn't know. Skydiving in Costa Rica is virtually unknown. This was the reason enthusiasts like Miguel had to go to Nicaragua to practice the sport. As a result, Donny's training program had to be creative. Paragliding on the other hand had come on the scene in recent years and there were many locations around. One that was close was the Santa Ana Pabellion Mountain. While Santa Ana is only a short distance from downtown San Jose, Donny still had to rent a four-wheel drive vehicle plus a driver/guide to get to the launch site, which was a small peak near the top of the mountain.

As they were packing up, Frank, a little worried asked, "Donny, are you sure about this? I don't see how this will help with learning about night diving."

"First I want to make sure you can maneuver the chute. I want to see if you can hit the LZ."

"Ok, I guess. How far is it?"

"Not far. We'll be there in an hour."

It turned out to be almost two hours. They got to the Santa Ana area in a half hour but it took another hour and a half to get up to the launch area.

The last half hour, there was no road and the driver had to stop many times to get his bearings. He basically followed ruts left by other enthusiasts.

When they reached the peak, they were 1800 meters up. Donny walked out to the edge of the peak and looked down.

He pointed to a large field off to the left and down and said to Frank,

"See that grassy area over there? That's the LZ. That's where we want to land. I'll go first to give you a read on the Thermals, then you can follow."

Frank, fighting the strong wind to keep his balance on the small perch said, "You mean you want me to jump alone? After you've gone?"

"Either that or wait till I come back up. That could be quite a while Frank. Look, it's not much different from jumping from a plane and these chutes are specifically designed for this type of jumping. If you ask me, it's easier than jumping out of a plane. There are over 100,000 people doing this every day. I'll give you a complete ground school brief and after that, you'll be chomping at the bit to go."

They went back to the 4X4 and unpacked the rented gear. Donny explained how the parapente was born in the basics of the ram air parachute with a bigger wing and a perfect aerodynamic side. He explained that the nylon wings are made of open cells in the front and closed on the back and how the air that blows into the cells and makes the wing rise up. He showed Frank how the harness is the control for steering the parapente with both hands. He cautioned Frank not to oversteer as that could cause a sudden loss of air and even control.

Then he showed Frank how to don the harness and adjust the chute so that it would easily flow out on the run. They made several dry runs till Donny was satisfied that Frank could do it.

Finally, it was time for Donny to give Frank a demonstration. Donny stood at the back of the peak. He put on his helmet and adjusted his shoulder and kneepads. He gave Frank a thumbs up and ran full speed off the edge of the peak. Frank watched and saw Donny rise up as the big chute caught a thermal. Then, he watched Donny turn to the right and then left and eventually glide effortlessly toward the LZ. Frank thought that it looked fun and was anxious to try it. His final thought as he ran down the slope was that he had taken leave of his senses but run he did. The training kicked in and he concentrated on controlling the chute and suddenly he was airborne. The feeling was one of exuberance and freedom. The valley below looked far away and peaceful. There was absolute silence. He could see the LZ and he jerked on the harness to turn right. Suddenly, he found himself falling too fast. He had jerked too hard. He corrected with a slight tug to the left and regained control. He made looping turns to practice. He was getting the hang of it. Now he could see Donny waiting below, but he was coming in too fast. He slowed his decent but too late. He hit the ground running but stumbled and fell in the muddy grass.

Before he could get up, he heard Donny yelling. "Frank, that was great."

Frank checked for broken bones and bruises. Finding none he got up, wiping mud off his face and chest.

Donny eagerly continued, "You looked like a pro. Wow! We have to work on a couple of things but I'll have you night jumping in no time."

The next few days, the process was repeated multiple times until it was almost monotonous for Frank. On the third day after another successful jump, they were riding back up the mountain, Donny said, "When we get back up, we'll take a break and send the driver down. Then we wait."

"For what?" Frank said.

"For it to get dark. We'll know it's time when the driver turns on his headlights down in the LZ. We have to finish this up. Dick is on me to get you ready and I think you're ready."

After the driver let them off, they sat around drinking water and smoking. They were able to see a spectacular sun setting in the west as they were making final checks of the equipment. The headlights of the 4X4 came on below, and Donny told Frank to follow him as close as possible just as he would be when they jumped from the plane. With that, he gave Frank a thumbs up and took off into the darkness.

I can't even see him, how am I supposed to stay close? Frank thought but ran down the slope as he was told. Once airborne, he felt better. He could see the ground lights all around the valley. He looked over towards the LZ and was able to make out the headlights. Then he saw Donny just ahead. Donny had brought a flashlight and was blinking it furiously because Frank was about to plow into him. Frank turned just in time avoiding a collision that could have been trouble for both of them. Donny kept the light on as they made a series of turns and maneuvers. The lights from the 4X4 served them well and they hit the ground without any further mishaps.

"A little close for comfort, eh, amigo?" Donny said as he wrapped an arm around Franks shoulder.

"Thank God you had that flashlight or I would have been toast," Frank said.

"Don't worry Frank. When we go for real, we'll have the moon to guide us. Dick told me so it must be so," Donny said laughingly as they stowed the gear and climbed into the vehicle for the ride back to San Jose.

They were ready.

CHAPTER 28

—■—

JUMP OFF

Six days later, Miguel was waiting outside of Dick's place a good two hours before the 8:00 Am Taca Airlines flight was set to leave. Dick emerged from his house dressed in a blazer, white shirt and gray slacks. In his hand, he carried a duffel bag in which he had packed a few necessities plus the "Doctor Bag" which contained all the material necessary for carrying out his objective of seducing his prey.

"Buenos Dios, Amigo, y gracias," Dick said as he accepted a café con leche Miguel had thoughtfully picked up for him on the way. It was early and he needed the caffeine. As Miguel put it in gear and pulled out, Dick asked, "Everything set?"

"Relax, amigo. The pilot's on standby and I talk to him every two hours. Weather looks great," Miguel said.

"What about Donny?"

"No problem, he's been training hard all week. Frank has become a star student. Donny said Frank is a natural, almost like he's done it before. He says they're ready. Oh, before I forget, I talked with Juanita last night. She put her lover on a bus yesterday and he's back on the island. Evidently, they had quite a weekend. Juanita says they never left her apartment. Anyway, he knows you are coming and is ready to help."

Dick felt a tinge of jealousy but quashed it and said, "Yeah, I met the kid at her apartment the other night. She seems to have control over him. Just in case, I brought along a little extra bribe money."

"Couldn't hurt", Miguel said as he pulled onto the Autopista that led to the airport.

As they pulled up to the passenger drop area, Dick noticed that the recent construction was nearly completed and how nice the airport complex was looking. After saying goodbye to Miguel and being reassured that he would be waiting on the southern shore of the lake with the SUV that would take them back to San Jose the next night, he made his way into the ticket counter area stopping off to pay his "salida" tax of $26.00 which the Costa Rican government collected from all travelers exiting the country. After getting his receipt, he got in the line for the Taca Airline ticket counter. Every bag that was going to be checked in was being searched by hand prior to proceeding to the counter. Since he only had carry-on, his bag would not be searched 'til he went through security. Once at the counter, he had to fill out a customs document of some sort. Once the ticket agent made sure he had paid his taxes and filled out his forms correctly, she printed his boarding pass. With a smile, told him to get in the security line, which was enormous. Dick waited for at least 20 minutes 'til it was his turn to take off his shoes, belt, jacket, and put his pocket change into a small wooden tray, which in turn went into the X-ray machines. His bag was also placed on the belt but was halted by the security screener who asked Dick to open it. Just then, Dick remembered that it was probably the needles and scalpels that was causing the problem.

Just great, he thought as the official asked him, "Are you a Doctor, Senor?"

Trying not to show too much relief, Dick smiled and said, *"Si, Yo soy Medico"*. To Dick's amazement, the official closed the bag, smiled and told him to have a nice flight. Thank God for lax Costa Rican security!

As he sat in the boarding area, he reviewed the plan in his mind. Juanita had assured him repeatedly this past week that the young nica guard was putty in her hands. Dick had met him in her apartment. He went over the plan with him over and over. In Spanish and English. They worked out pre-arranged signals. Dick was convinced the kid could and would do it. He was wild for Juanita. Poor kid, he thought.

The Taca agent announcing that the 8:00 AM flight was ready to board interrupted his thoughts. He got in line with the other passengers, showed his boarding pass and passport and found his seat in the business section. The doctor would be proud he thought as he slid into his comfortable seat.

The flight took an hour. Dick felt that they never got over 10,000 feet as he could see the rolling hills and farmland the whole way. After they landed, the passengers were directed to go to the customs and immigration area. Dick ducked into the nearest restroom where he killed enough time to assure himself that all the passengers from his flight had passed through to the customs area.

Walking out of the restroom, with a boarding pass in hand, he looked like any other passenger waiting for a flight out of Nicaragua. He lost himself in a crowd and moved along 'til he came to a bank of TV monitors showing arrivals and departures. He quickly saw that the Taca flight from Los Angeles was on time and due in at 10:00 AM. He looked at his watch. It was now 9:25. He noted that the flight was coming in at gate 6. He was at gate 4. He casually walked with other passengers to gate 6. When he got to the gate, he saw another crowded boarding area waiting on a flight to San Jose, Costa Rica. Evidently, the good doctor's flight from LAX would continue on down to Costa Rica. Small world, Dick thought.

He sat down, pulled a book from his bag and started reading. He appeared to all the world as just another passenger waiting for his flight to be called. As he sat there, he stole glances around the boarding area and noticed three official looking Nicaraguan men. All three were in suits but were obliviously packing some kind of heat. They talked amongst themselves and had some kind of radios with them that they constantly spoke into. They did not fit in with the passengers, Dick thought. Maybe these guys were here because of Cummings. They certainly fit the bill.

Dick's thoughts were interrupted by a flight announcement, first in Spanish and then in English that Taca flight 807 from Los Angeles had landed and would soon be deplaning passengers at gate 6. Dick put his book down, rose out of his seat, stretched and looked out the big windows. It was then that he spotted a 737 approaching the gate. Men with long flashlights were guiding the plane into its reserved berth at the gate. Dick glanced towards where he last saw the three officials and they were gone. He then started fishing around his bags just like the majority of the other anxious passengers were doing.

The engines made a final whine as the pilot shut them down, the jet way moved into position. The gate agent opened the door to the jet way and rushed down the carpeted path to the plane. A short while later, passengers started emerging, but they were kind of looking back into the jet way as they came out. Then Dick saw the three officials plus a blonde American struggling between two of them. The American was shouting and it was hard to make out what he was saying but Dick distinctly heard something about demanding to see the American Consulate. The Nicaraguan officials just kept going and Dick saw them go through an unmarked door not far from the gate area. That was the last Dick saw of the presumed Dr. Golightly.

Giving one last stretch, Dick calmly picked up his bags, took out his "other" passport and joined in with the coach passengers exiting the jet way. No one noticed and if they did, all they saw was the blonde American whom they had seen on the plane. The passengers, who had seen the scuffle, were well in front and had no idea what had happened after the American had left with the three officials.

The passengers from Taca 807 wound up at Nicaraguan Customs. Dick patiently stood in line with everyone else. When it was his turn, he presented his documents to the agent who simply asked why he was visiting Nicaragua. Dick replied something about his needing to see a patient. The bored agent, stamped his phony passport and Dick, as Dr. Eric Golightly, passed through to the waiting throng of relatives, friends and taxi hustlers. He noticed 3 Nicaraguan men standing together dressed in white shirts and black trousers. He noticed them because one of them was pointing at him and holding a picture. As Golightly would do, Dick looked confused and arrogant at the same time. One of the men then held up a sign that read

"Dr. Golightly". When he saw it, Dick held up one hand while holding the bags in the other and gave a nod.

Two of the men were husky, with mustaches and approaching middle age. Dick was relieved to see that the other one was Julio. All three approached him. One of the older ones, obviously the leader, said, "Dr. Golightly?"

Dick quickly replied, "Yes, I'm Golightly, you guys from Hernandez?" he said in a slight New England yuppie accent.

"Si, Señor, you are to come with us," the leader said as he reached out and took one of Dick's bags.

Outside, Dick had to immediately take off his coat. The temperature was a good 20 degrees hotter than San Jose. The younger man offered to carry his other bag and Dick accepted looking for some sign of recognition from Juanita's boyfriend but did not get one. There was a black Ford Excursion waiting at the curb. Without a word, they piled in and rapidly pulled away.

CHAPTER 29

———— ■ ————

ON THE ISLAND

T he younger guy (Julio) drove and one of the goons sat up front
with him. Dick and the leader sat in the back. Dick asked if it was
always this hot in Managua, to which he got a *"Si Señor"* from the
leader who then reached up and adjusted the rear passenger air vent. The
cool air felt great and realizing he wasn't going to get much conversation,
Dick settled back to enjoy the ride. The road leading away from the airport
was a highway with occasional stoplights. Off to the left, in the distance,
Dick could see some scattered modern high-rises but no real skyline for
what he thought might be the downtown area. He then remembered that
there had been a severe earthquake about five or six years ago. Most of the
old downtown had been destroyed. They continued on the highway and
then suddenly turned off with the driver screeching to a stop alongside
the road.

"Why are we stopping?" Dick said with a hint of arrogance and panic.

"Not to worry, Senor Doctor, we have to blindfold you from here 'til we
get to the house."

"What? No! You can't do that. Do you know who I am? This is outrageous.
Take me back to the airport. I demand you take me back to the airport now!"

With this, the leader slapped Dick across the face and said "We don't
have time for your stupid outburst gringo, now put this on." He handed
Dick a blindfold. With a shocked look on his face, Dick reluctantly put it on
saying something about reporting the incident to the leader's superiors. The

last thing Dick saw before they pulled the blindfold down was the leader's big grin. He then felt hands guiding him back into the vehicle.

It was about a two-hour ride to the next stop, the boat dock but Dick, as Dr. Golightly was not supposed to know this. The door on Dick's side opened and more hands reached in and pulled him out.

Dick said, "Oh, good we're here, can I take this ridiculous thing off now?"

"No Señor, we are only transferring you to another vehicle. Leave it on."

"Another vehicle! Look, hasn't this gone on long enough? Why all the cloak and dagger?"

The leader voice's came back, "Senor, we are following orders, now get on the boat."

"Boat! What boat? Are you kidding? This is crazy!"

"Señor, do I have to hit you again?"

Dick's body language gave a sign of resignation and he sheepishly said, "No."

Rough hands guided him into the boat and then to a seat. It was hot and Dick could feel the warmth of the hot sun. He heard the sounds of orders being shouted and rope being thrown and a motor starting. He felt movement as they pulled away from the dock. Finally, they were moving and the breeze provided him with some relief from the hot sun.

The throaty sound of the twin engines and the pitch of the craft as it sped through the water told Dick that he was on a cigarette boat which explained the rough ride he was feeling. These boats were built for speed, not comfort. As bumpy as it was, the refreshing breeze and cool spray felt good.

They rode along like this for about 30 minutes when suddenly he felt the bow dip and the engines throttled back. Someone, probably Julio, came near him and gently removed his blindfold. The bright sun was such that he could barely see. He squinted and blinked as he slowly regained his sight. He could see that they were approaching a dock where other boats, including a military type swamp boat, were berthed. The short dock led to a piece of land that shot straight up. He could make out stairs that had been carved into the volcanic rock. He looked up but the rise was so high, he could not discern where the top was.

Now they were maneuvering the boat alongside the dock and a deckhand was catching rope and securing it to cleats on the dock. The leader jumped off first and barked to the younger man in Spanish that he was to grab the doctor's bags and escort him off the boat. The kid quickly picked up Dick's bags. Dick rose as the kid came up to him and gently placed a hand on his arm as if to help him up. Dick thought he felt a small squeeze which reassured him that Juanita's lover was still on his side. They scurried off the boat and made their way to the rough stairs. The climb wasn't as bad as it could have been as they only went up one flight to a landing that led them off at the entrance to a cave. They entered the well-lighted cave and Dick found himself standing with the three men at an elevator door, which opened, by a remote held by one of the goons. They entered and Dick watched as one of them pushed a button marked two. The old elevator protested and creaked but in short order the door opened to a courtyard that was the center of the castle. It's exactly like the photos, Dick thought.

A well-dressed couple that had just come out of one of the doors to their right interrupted his thoughts. The balding short man was smiling as he strode toward Dick. He extended his hand which Dick took as he returned the smile.

"Doctor Golightly, I presume," he said while chuckling at his little Dr. Livingston type joke in his heavily accented English.

Dick smiled and replied, "Señor."

"Oh forgive me, please allow me to introduce myself, I am Enrique Hernandez and this charming creature, is my wife, Maria. I am to be your patient, Doctor."

"Oh, I see. Yes, very well. Mr. Hernandez, this is all quite irregular. What is it that you want done? Where am I to operate? Can I see the facilities?"

Ricky smiled and said, "So many questions, Doctor. Everything will be answered but let's get you settled in. You look like you could use a freshening up, is that how you say it?"

"Well yes, I would appreciate that, the ride over was a bit out of the ordinary. Is all the cloak and dagger necessary?"

"So sorry, Señor Doctor, but there are bad people that would love to get their hands on me and my Maria. I hope you understand. Now let's get you to your room so you can relax a bit."

He turned to the leader and told him in Spanish to have one of his people escort the Doctor to one of the guest rooms. The man nodded and turned to the kid with the bags and handed him what looked like a room key.

The kid gave a quick nod, looked at Dick, said *"Vamos Señor"* and took off toward one of the arches that surrounded the courtyard. Dick gave a halfhearted wave to his new patient and rushed off to catch up with the kid.

He caught up with the kid, Juanita's lover, who now waiting at the elevator. He was about to say something when the kid put a finger to his lips and slowly shook his head back and forth. They rode the elevator up a couple of floors and exited into a hallway that could have been any Hilton or Marriott on the planet. Quickly, they were in front of an unmarked door. The kid slid the key in and before he knew it, Dick was standing in an upscale hotel room that could rival any suite in New York or Los Angeles.

Dick again started to say something but the kid once again put a finger to his lips and motioned for Dick to follow him into the small bathroom. Once there, the kid reached in and turned on the shower, flushed the toilet and turned on all the faucets. Even then he whispered as he said, "Señor Dick, all the rooms are bugged. You must not say anything. Everything is ready. You are to wash and unpack. Then someone will come get you for lunch. The operation is to be late this afternoon. Then of course, your friends arrive tonight at 1:00 am as planned, No?"

Dick looked at him with some relief and thanked him, asked if the boat they would be using would be the swamp boat he saw at the dock. The kid said that it would be but he must now get back as he didn't want to arouse and suspicions. He smiled at Dick and quickly left.

Alone, Dick made a quick recon of the room. The window afforded a great lake view but no escape unless you were Spiderman because there was at least a 200 ft. drop straight down to the rocks that lined the water's edge.

He then put his medical bag on the bed. He took out the serum, the syringes, scalpels, the medications, the bandages and other medical tools. He was troubled that he hadn't somehow figured out a way to smuggle in a handgun of some sort. He'd have to wait for Donny who was supposed to be bringing him one. He strode around the room once again looking for anything else he could use. He checked on the bathroom, took some washcloths and towels and stuffed them in his medical bag. While there, he splashed some water on his face and touched up the light make up Juanita had applied. He took off his jacket and lay down for a quick nap. No more than fifteen minutes had gone by when he was jarred awake by the ringing phone. He grabbed it and said hello in the voice of the snotty Doctor.

"Yes, Doctor, A man is coming up for you. Lunch is ready." A voice told him.

A moment later, he heard a knock at the door. He got up and strode across the room and opened the door to find one of the goons smiling and gesturing that he should go with him. He went back to the bed, retrieved his bag and put on his blazer. They went back to the elevator and Dick noticed that the man pushed the highest button on the panel, which was two buttons above his floor. Once again the elevator creaked and protested but opened to a roof top level that took in all the majesty of the castle. To his left, he saw commanding views of the lake. Behind him and before him rose tall turrets that provided excellent lookout posts. To his right, there was a wall with cut outs that looked down into the central courtyard. The area just in front of him had been remodeled to resemble an outdoor café. There were four tables with colorful umbrellas sitting on an Astroturf type of carpet. Since they were so high up, there was a gentle breeze. The blazing Nicaraguan sun was still hot but under the shade, it was actually quite pleasant. As Dick approached the table where Ricky and Maria Hernandez were sitting, Ricky rose and greeted him.

"The accommodations are to your liking, Senor?" Enrique said.

"Um, very nice, thank you, er Ricky is it?"

With a big laugh, Enrique said, "Si Senor Doctor, you can call me Ricky or should we go with the more dashing American name of Rick? No, I like Ricky. Now, what should I call you, Doctor?"

"Eric is fine," Dick, said.

"Very good then, it's Eric and you, of course, remember Maria?" indicating his wife seated to his left.

"Of course, good afternoon, Maria."

Maria nodded with a small smile.

"Please, please, sit down Eric," Ricky said indicating the chair across from him.

As Dick sat, a waiter appeared from nowhere and pushed in his chair, removed the napkin and with a flourish, placed it in Dick's lap. The lunch consisted of a small chilled salad followed by a Chilean sea bass that was the possibly the freshest Dick had ever tasted, all served with a delicious white wine. Over coffee and a delicious flan desert, they talked about the coming procedure.

Dick, as Doctor Golightly asked Ricky exactly what he wanted to accomplish.

"Very simple, Eric, I want to change how I look. I will be moving to a new city and I just want not to be recognized. Oh, and Maria here wants what you call a nose job, no?" He said this with a small chuckle as Maria smiled and blushed.

"Well Ricky, what you're asking shouldn't be too difficult. It's amazing what a small adjustment to the cheekbones and the nose can do. That coupled with a change in hair color and or facial hair can make it so that your own mother wouldn't recognize you."

"Eric, I have some questions," Ricky said.

"Sure, go ahead, Ricky."

"Well, ah, what about the pain?"

Dick gave a reassuring smile and said, "During the procedure, you're knocked out. You won't feel a thing. Afterward, as your face heals, there is some discomfort but that can be managed by pain pills which I will give you."

"Well, that's good, how long before the bandages come off?"

"Not long, about four days, then there is some discoloration but that goes away in about a week."

"That sounds better than I expected. So I could travel ten days after the operation?"

"I don't see why not," Dick said.

"Just how long does the procedure take?"

"Not long, a couple of hours, then another hour before you wake up."

"Why is it that you didn't bring along an Anesthesiologist?"

"Most Doctors would, Ricky. Unlike most Doctors, I am also trained in administering General Anesthesia. I think it's one of the reasons your people chose me for this job." Dick said surprising even himself.

"Well, you have certainly answered all of my questions. Maria?"

Maria smiled and said, "Ricky says my nose is too big. What do you think, Doctor Eric?"

"You have a beautiful nose Maria. But I can give you a slightly smaller one that will only serve to enhance the rest of your face."

To this, she just gave a shrug and smile. Ricky rose and asked if Dick (the Doctor) would like to see the room they had set up for him.

"Yes, I would very much like that," Dick said.

With that, he too got up and they all walked back to the elevator. This time, they only went down one level. The door opened on a luxurious suite that Ricky explained was where he and Maria were staying. Off the living area, there were four doors leading to various bedrooms. Ricky strode to one, opened it and waved to Dick (Dr. Golightly) to enter. Dick was surprised to see that the room had been set up as a typical exam room like one might see in any doctor's office in the U.S. There was an adjustable gurney that was big enough to double as a bed. One whole wall consisted of a counter with a built in sink and cabinets and drawers that probably contained bandages and other medical necessities. Overhead was a surgical lamp that would rival most operating rooms. On the counter were stacked sheets and pillows.

"Well, Senor Eric, what do you think of our little hospital room?"

"Rather impressive actually, I didn't expect this. It's quite complete."

CHAPTER 30

———————————■———————————

JOURNEY TO LIBERIA

While Dick was having lunch and inspecting the hospital facilities, Miguel, Donny, Carlos and Frank were rounding the last bend in the road that would eventually bring them into Liberia in the northwest province of Guanacaste, not far from the Nicaraguan border. They had made good time since leaving San Jose that morning. In the rainy season, the trip could take five hours but it was dry and they had made it in four. Miguel had rented an SUV for the occasion, which gave them plenty of room for them and their equipment.

As more and more tourists flocked to Costa Rica for its pristine beaches and rain forests on the Pacific side, Liberia and its airport had grown tremendously in the past five years. It had been expanded to accept wide body passenger jets from the states. The tourists loved it because they could now avoid the hassle of San José and the long and rough ride to the coast.

While Miguel drove, the others went over the plan. Donny wasn't taking any chances that someone didn't understand their job and when to do it. They also checked the equipment. Donny was glad Miguel had thought to obtain lightweight flack vests. The weapons consisted of four Beretta 9 MM 1/2X28 handguns fixed with AWC suppressors, a good supply of Black Hills 124 jacketed hollow point ammo and Israeli combat knives with sheaths.

Night sky diving military parachutes were also in the back. Once at the hanger, they would pack and re-pack them. They all wore black and would don web gear later.

"*Mira, Donny,*" Miguel said.

Donny looked up and saw that they were approaching the airport area. There were big signs directing cars to arrivals and departures but just before the final entrance, Miguel turned off and took a side road that was used by cargo trucks and vehicles for other airport related business. The road skirted the runway and was sprinkled with outbuildings and hangers. At one hanger, Miguel turned in and pulled up to a guard. They spoke in Spanish and the guard made a call. Satisfied, he opened the gate, gave Miguel directions and allowed them to enter. The hanger's front faced the road they had just left and the back faced the airport's taxiway that led to the main runway. As they parked, Donny noted the time. It was 4 Pm, which meant they had about 8 hours before take-off. Plenty of time for rest and rehearsal, Donny thought.

A trim man of about 40 dressed in khaki shorts and a white pilot's shirt approached the SUV. When he spotted Miguel, a wide grin appeared on his face and he jogged the rest of the way. Miguel smiled back and they shook hands and embraced. After a few exchanges in Spanish, Miguel turned to Donny, Frank and Carlos and said, "Gentlemen, allow me to introduce you to my friend Filipe, who will be your pilot."

They shook hands all around and Filipe asked if they wanted to stow their gear. Donny went to the rear of the SUV and opened the cargo hatch showing a full load. Without a word, they decided to unload and everyone grabbed their gear and followed Filipe into a side door of the massive hanger.

The place was deserted save one aircraft. It was a Cessna 208 Caravan Cargomaster. Because of its huge rear cargo door, it was very popular with sky diving enthusiasts. It had a top speed of 184 knots, which would easily get them to target in an hour. Donny had made many jumps from this type of aircraft and any trace of apprehension he had with Miguel's choice of pilot was immediately erased. Donny walked around the aircraft looking for oil leaks or other signs of wear and could find none. After a complete search, he nodded his approval towards Miguel and Filipe who looked relieved because he was due the second half of his flight fee upon Donny's approval. Donny was so impressed that he decided to pay Filipe now instead of waiting till they were over the drop zone.

"Nice ship," he said as he handed over a large wad of bills.

Startled, the pilot said, "Gracias, Senor. What time do you want to leave tonight?"

Donny scratched his stubble and said, "We need to be over the target at 12:50 AM."

Filipe who'd been briefed on the target and its exact whereabouts said,

"In that case, Senor Donny, we need to leave here at 11:45PM. I have to file a flight plan. I will make it seem as if we are flying over the lake to Managua. While I do that, why don't you and your men settle in. There are bathrooms and a small kitchen over in that area," he said as he pointed to a corner of the hanger. "The fridge is stocked with sandwiches and soft drinks."

Donny nodded his thanks and as Filipe turned to go, Donny perhaps having second thoughts shouted, "Hey, wait. How do I know you'll come back?"

"All you need to know *Señor* is that my father, who is a retired school teacher living in San José lost $50,000 with those crooked cousins."

Donny nodded and said, "Good enough for me, see you when you get back."

Donny turned to Miguel, "Good man you found us."

"Gracias, Donny. Filipe is originally from Panama and worked as an instructor with the US Army until they closed their bases in Panama. He runs a good sky diving school here. The best equipment, rigorous training, he won't let you jump 'till he's sure you've received the necessary ground training."

Miguel looked at his watch and said, "It's about 5:00 now. You have almost 8 hours to kill. I will leave you to get to our rendezvous in a couple of hours. Meanwhile, I need a siesta to rest up from the drive."

Donny said, "Good, you have the co-ordinates for the rendezvous?"

Miguel nodded. It had been agreed earlier that they would meet in the swampy area just north of the village of Mexico, not far from where Enrique and his wife caught the boat to the island. The co-ordinates had been gleaned from the information provided by the satellite.

"If all goes well, we should be pulling in there around 2:00 am. When we get close to the co-ordinates, we will flash a beam once. You flash back twice. Got it?"

Miguel told him he would be there and then excused himself, as he wanted to get at least two or three hours sleep before he had to leave.

------■------

CHAPTER 31

SCRUBS

D ick was back in his room changing into the scrubs that certainly made him look more like a surgeon than even he thought possible. The good Dr. Golightly would be proud he thought as he looked at the completed product in the mirror. He glanced at his watch. It was almost 6 O'clock. They would come for him soon, but he had to stall. He didn't want for his part to be over and done with, only for him to have to wait two or three hours before the rescue team arrived.

The knock came and Dick opened the door to see that the older goon had been sent to get him.

"I just need a moment to collect some of my things."

The guard nodded and waited as Dick scurried about the room collecting his bag and his mostly black change of clothes which he would put on after the "operation."

Once ready, he joined the guard who grabbed one of his bags and started off towards the elevator. As Dick scurried to catch up, he had an idea to stall. Pretty good he thought to himself as the elevator ground to a stop and let them out on Ricky's floor.

As soon as Ricky opened the door, Dick, as Dr. Golightly rushed in while simultaneously talking up a storm. "Rick, what time did we finish eating earlier? Can you remember?"

A little taken aback, Ricky said, "Er, uh about 2 O'clock I think Senor Doctor. Is there a problem?"

"Just a small one, Ricky, this procedure requires that the patient can't eat for 12 hours prior to the operation."

"Yes, but well, Doctor, that would make it 2 am before you could start."

"Hmm, can you remember what you had?" Dick said while stroking his chin and looking very deep in thought.

"It was just a piece of fish and some wild rice and vegetables."

"Good! That's what I thought," Dick/Golightly said with a snap of his fingers. "With fish, we can slash that time to nine hours which means we can start at 11:00."

"Very good Doctor but what do we do in the meantime?"

"Glad you asked," Dick said as he rummaged through his bag and pulled out a small laptop computer. "Have a seat, Ricky."

Like many, Dick had discovered the wonders of the Internet in his later years. He was amazed at what it could do. At first, he just used it for email and chat rooms with his ex-military buddies. As he learned more, he found he could research just about anything. Need a recipe to spice up that chicken dinner you have in mind? Google it. Need driving directions to a place you've never been before? Do a Map Quest. Need a last minute gift for that hard to please niece who likes cats? Shop on Amazon. Need to find out how plastic surgery works? Do a search and come up with a computer program that lets the patient see what he or she would look like with some small adjustments. Dick had done just that and had downloaded a program that with the aid of a digital camera could make Ricky Hernandez look like Rock Hudson.

"Ok Doctor, I'm sitting, now what?" Ricky said with just a hint of irritation in his voice.

"First, we're going to take a picture of you and one of Maria," Dick said as he pulled out his small digital camera. "Then through the magic of computer technology, you can see what you'll look like after we perform tonight's procedure."

With that, Maria's interest rose and her face lit up as she said, "I wanna go first. Can I go first? Pleeease, Rickeeey."

"I don't care who goes first, let's just get started. How long will this take, Doctor?"

"Not long, an hour for each of you, but why rush it? You know we can't start till 11:00. That means when we finish this initial consultation, you'll still have a couple of hours to kill."

Rick stood and waved for his wife to take his seat. Maria giggled and eagerly sat down. Ricky let out a sigh and rolled his eyes. Smiling, Dick positioned her and hooked up the wire from the computer to the camera. Her image would appear almost instantly when he took the shot. He asked Ricky to stand behind her while holding up a white sheet, lined up the shot and started to snap away but she was posing this way and that.

"Maria, no smile, this is not for the newspapers. It's more of a driver's license picture."

"Ok Senor Doctor. I no smile."

He got off a couple of good straight shots and then moved to the side for the profile. "Ok, that's it for you. Let see what the computer has to say."

Dick went to the laptop and typed in commands, and entered, and waited and typed some more. To a casual observer, he looked like he knew what he was doing. Maria was standing behind him with a look of great anticipation while Ricky was still staring out the window. Maria let out a scream when she saw her pictures come up on the format Dick had been loading them into.

"What now, Maria? What is the problem?" Ricky said.

"Mira, Ricky, its me." She said as she pointed to the computer screen.

He came over to where she was standing and looked at the image on the screen and sure enough, her pictures were there front and side.

"Looks like a mug shot, mi amor." He chided and she immediately gave him a mock punch in the arm. He smiled, grabbed her and gave her a big hug.

Like a couple of teenagers, Dick thought as he continued entering commands one of which was the icon for the human nose. Up popped another screen that displayed noses of celebrities like Jennifer Lopez, Meg Ryan, Helen Hunt and Sarah Jessica Parker. Maria had to stifle a scream as she gazed at the possibilities. Putting on his best Doctor bedside manner, Dick asked Maria to choose a nose.

Breathlessly, Maria pointed to the J- Lo nose on the screen. Dick smiled, entered a couple of commands and viola, up popped a computer likeness of Maria with the nose of Jennifer Lopez. Dick thought it made her look different but not all that different. Maria however was ecstatic as she anxiously said, "Si Doctor Eric, that is the one for me, please?"

"No problem, Maria, it's the one you shall have. I'll just save it in the computer for later use this evening," he said as he hit a couple of more keys.

Dick thought to himself that this was going good. In another life, he could be a pretty good con man. In any case, these two were hooked.

"Ok Ricky, it's your turn. Have a seat."

After he was seated, he asked Maria to hold up the sheet like Ricky had done for her. He posed Ricky for front and side shots and snapped away like a pro. After the computer brought up Ricky's images, he suggested a modest changes in the chin, nose and hairline that altered Ricky's appearance dramatically. Both Ricky and Maria were impressed. As Dick saved the changes, he realized that if the real doctor had made it here, it was a distinct possibility that Ricky would have been able to get away without ever having to worry about being recognized.

"What happens now, Doctor?" Ricky asked.

Dick looked at his watch and saw that it was 8:30. "You rest, while I go get something to eat. I need the energy. I'll be back a little before 11:00. In the meantime, I'd like you both to take one of these," he said as he handed each a small pill.

"What are they?"

"Just a relaxant that will calm you for the procedure"

"Ok, you want me to get the guard to take you to the kitchen?"

"Please, I'm famished," Dick said thinking that he really was.

The guard who had been summoned by a phone call from Ricky arrived and Dick left with him.

CHAPTER 32

PACKING UP

Donny, Carlos and Frank were sitting around after digesting ham and cheese sandwiches, cokes and chips. They were killing time. Donny noted it was coming up on 9 O'clock. He got up, stretched, yawned and shuffled over to the cot in the corner where Miguel was catching a nap.

"Ok, amigo, time to rise and shine," he said as he shook his shoulder.

Miguel turned, looked at Donny and said, "That time already?"

Donny told him yes and with that, Miguel got up and headed for the little bathroom to splash some water on his face. When he emerged, the other three were standing together. Miguel hugged Donny and Frank and shook Carlos the Nicaraguans hand. His parting words were, "I'll see you caballeros on the beach around 2:00am. If I don't see your signal, I'll flash my lights every couple of minutes. Good luck." With that, he was out the door.

As they stood there looking after Miguel, Donny brought them back to reality by saying, "Guys, we've got like two and a half hours to check the gear, pack the chutes and go over the mission one more time. Let's get cracking."

They drew their equipment from the pile on the floor. They cleaned the Berettas, checked the mechanisms, re-attached the suppressors, and loaded extra magazines so that running out of ammo in a firefight would not be a problem. They prepared their web gear and secured everything with tape so as not to make noise when they would be jumping and hitting the ground on the run. Combat knives were sharpened and sheathed to thighs and ankles for quick access. Grenades also had to be taped to the web harness with special care. The last thing they needed was a grenade going off while still strapped to someone's chest. When completed, each man had made his little pile that would enable him to pick everything up and strap it on in record time.

Then they went over to where the parachutes were piled. Donny had put together a long table left over from construction material consisting of a couple of doors and carpenters' horses. The three of them stretched out the first of three chutes. It was a SET10 Military Airborne Canopy with a 7-TU steering configuration. Not the latest in parachute technology but definitely a proven commodity. As long as the wind was not a problem, they would be able to steer their chutes into the target. Each man checked and double-checked each other's chute. Donny checked all the completed chutes.

Satisfied, they added the chutes to their respective piles and then sat on the piles while Donny grilled them on their respective chores and times.

"Carlos, once you hit the courtyard, where do you go?"

"Clear the area of any guards. Then meet at the elevator."

"Good. What about you Frank?"

"Take up a firing position to cover Carlos' and your landing."

"Once I land, I'll cover you and gather up the chutes and stuff them in the trash bin. Then we wait near the elevator for the signal from the kid."

Time must have moved faster than they thought. Filipe who had returned to do his pre-flight interrupted them.

"Hey Filipe, how much time before we load?" Donny asked.

"Fifteen minutes and I need to go over the flight plan with you."

"Ok guys, you heard the man. Saddle up."

Donny was ready first. He ambled over to where Filipe was standing with a clipboard. As the others finished preparing themselves, they boarded the plane.

"What's up?" Donny asked as he approached the pilot.

"Light winds in the area but they should dissipate by the time we arrive. What I'm most concerned about is the moon. It's pretty bright tonight. I just hope they don't have a wide-awake guard peering up in the sky. It will help you if I cut my engine and glide when we approach the drop area. That gives the three of you about ten seconds to exit the ship. Your signal will be the lack of sound when I cut the engine. You ok with that?"

Donny who hadn't had a drink or been near a casino for almost two weeks said, "It's exactly what we trained for. I'll inform my guys."

Filipe patted him on the shoulder and said, "Good luck, amigo. You pull this off and we'll tie one on down in San Jose. On me."

Donny smiled at the pilot and said, "Better bring your A game. It's what I'm best at."

With that they boarded the plane. Filipe did a quick check of his systems and started his engines. He radioed the tower and asked for permission to taxi out to the runways. Permission was immediately granted.

The Cessna rolled out of the hanger at precisely 11:45.

CHAPTER 33

■

THE PROCEDURE

After having a sandwich in the now empty rooftop café, Dick needed a smoke. He looked up from what was left of his meal and noticed that the guard had been changed. Juanita's lover now stood by the elevator. He gave Dick a wink. Dick gave a small wave for him to come over. It was almost time for him to go back to the suite to begin the procedure. The guard approached and Dick told him he needed to stretch his legs and grab a quick smoke before going back up to the suite.

"Si Señor, we can take a stroll around the edge, in front of the old gun emplacements."

Dick rose and followed Julio who led him through a cutout in the wall that led to a path that circumvented the entire top portion of the castle. Once they were out of sight, Dick shook out a cigarette and offered one to Julio who readily accepted. They stopped to light up and Dick whispered, "Can we talk?"

"*No hay problema, Señor Dick*. It's why I bring you out here. No cameras. *Bueno, no?*"

"Perfect. Ok, I'll go down to the suite in a few minutes. I should be done in an hour and half or so. By then, I'll have what I came for. What happens then?'

"At 1:00, I will knock on the door one time Señor. Because I am the junior guard, the old ones assign me the night duty outside your door. It is I who will be outside the door. I will bring your amigos to you."

"Yes, one time, one knock. One o'clock. Ok? The boat ready?" Dick asked.

"Si, I checked it just before I come on duty. About one hour ago," he said as he held up the ignition key.

Dick stubbed out his cigarette, smiled and told Julio he was ready to go down to the suite. Julio led him back to the elevator, which took them back to the third level. A quick knock and as they entered the suite, the first thing Dick saw was Ricky and Maria sitting on the couch looking very relaxed and happy. The pills had kicked in, Dick thought.

"*Buenos Noches*, Doctor Eric," Ricky said with a slur while Maria could just manage a smile and a lethargic wave of the hand. The strong relaxant had done its work Dick thought.

"Ok, who's first?" Dick asked.

Maria looked scared so Ricky said he would go first.

"Ok, Rick, why don't you go on in change into the hospital gown on the gurney. I'll be right in. With that, Ricky rose and half stumbled into the other room.

Dick dug in his bag, pulled out the bottle of pills, turned to Maria and said, "Take another one of these so you'll be ready when it's your turn, Maria." In her state, she readily complied and even gave him a sexy bedroom eye smile.

Dick chuckled, told her to just relax and it would be her turn soon. She laid down on the couch and was just about out as Dick pulled a blanket over her. Dick knew that she would actually be out for at least four hours giving him more than enough time to work on Ricky, get the diamonds, and get off the island.

Next, he grabbed his bag, went into the exam room and started his preparations. As Ricky lay back on the gurney, Dick made a show out of scrubbing his hands and carefully laying out all of his medical equipment on a small tray next to his patient who seemed fairly impressed.

"What's that needle for, Doctor Eric," Rick asked as Dick laid it on the tray.

"It's a local so you won't experience any pain."

"Good, I can't handle pain," Ricky mumbled.

Finished, Dick said, "Well, we're just about ready to start. You ready?"

Dick swabbed Ricky's arm with cotton soaked in iodine. He then prepared the needle by injecting the head into the bottle of serum he had brought along for the occasion. Once it was about a quarter full, he pulled it out and then squirted some into the air. A common misconception is that truth serum is actually called truth serum. It is not. Most drugs used for the purpose of obtaining information from unwilling subjects include ethanol, scopolamine and sodium pentothal. What Dick brought along for this job was Sodium Pentothal. This sedative interferes with better judgment but its drawback is its effects only last about 30 minutes. From his contacts at the DEA, Dick knew he would also have to gain Ricky's confidence. While it does work, the subject is not likely to reveal information to a stranger just asking where something is. Dick needed to trick Hernandez. He'd been working on an idea for that.

Dick injected the needle into Ricky's arm and watched as the liquid drained into his patient. He looked at Ricky who seemed a little confused but at the same time, relaxed. Not surprisingly, it only took about five seconds for Ricky to go out. Dick gathered up his equipment and put it all back in the bag. Ok, here goes, he thought.

Switching to Spanish he said as he gently touched Ricky's shoulder, "*Primo Enrique, ponte las pilas.*" (Cousin Ricky. Wake up.)

"*Quien es?*" Ricky mumbled." (Who is it?)

"*Ese es Memo, Enrique.*" (It's Memo, Ricky.)

"*No es posible. Usted estaba en San José. En la cárcel.*" (It's not possible, you're in San Jose. In Jail.)

"*Si, corecto pero yo escapé. Está mañana.*" Yes, that's right but I escaped this morning."

"*Bueno! Memo, eso es fantastico.*" (Good Memo, very good)

"*Gracias Enrique. Yo necesito su ayuda.*" (Thanks Ricky. I need your help.)

"*Que puedo hacer?*" (What can I do.)?

"*Yo necesito mi dinero para salir de Centro America a Europa.*" (I need my money to leave Central America for Europe.)

"*No hay problema, Memo. Dile a Maria y ella te dará la plata.*" (No problem, tell Maria and she will get you the money).

Dick looked at his watch. He had already used 10 minutes. He had to step it up.

"Enrique, Maria esta dormida y no es posible para mi levantarla." (She is asleep and it's not possible to wake her).

"Si, Yo entiendo. Dame la maleta a mí." (Yes, I understand, get the case for me).

"Si, pero donde esta?" (Yes, but where is it?)

"Usted lo sabe. En el armario. No recuerda?" (You know, in the closet, you don't remember?)

"Si, si, yo recuerdo. El armario." (Yes, I remember. The closet).

Dick rushed to the next room opened the closet and there was the black briefcase. He thought this was too easy. Then he noticed the combination locks on the top.

He took the briefcase back to the exam room and switching back to Spanish, said, *"Enrique, Yo tengo la maleta pero no recuerdo la combinación."* (I have the case but I don't remember the combination)

"Idiota! Es el compleanos de mi esposa." (You idiot. It's the birthday of my wife)

"Si, si. Yo soy muy estupido, Espera." (Yes, I am very stupid. Wait)

Dick went back to where Maria was sleeping and looked for a purse or wallet. Finding none, he rushed into the master bedroom and tore open drawers and pulled apart bed linen. Frustrated, he stood in the room and looked at his watch. He was running out of time. The light from the bathroom caught his eye. The bathroom! Women also keep lipstick, creams and eye shadow in their purses! He rushed into the bathroom and there it was just sitting on the counter. He ripped it open and found the wallet. Inside the wallet was a Costa Rican driver's license, which had a date of birth, September 21, 1972.

He went back to the case. There were two locks, one on the left, one on the right. He tried 921 on the left side and it worked! He entered the same number for the lock on the right but it didn't pop. Ok, he thought and then tried 212. No luck. He tried 972 and viola, it too sprung open.

He was looking at the contents of a typical briefcase. It was full of papers, a checkbook, address book, pens, keys, cards and a map but no diamonds. He turned it over and most everything fell out. No diamonds. He sat on the closed toilet seat in the luxurious bathroom and heard a moan. He looked at his watch and realized that the effectiveness of the drug he used on Ricky was wearing off. He rushed back to the exam room where Ricky was starting to stir. First he grabbed the chloroform, soaked it in gauze and held it to Ricky's nose and mouth.

Ricky went back out. Dick had bought some more time but not much. He went back to the closet and checked to make sure there wasn't another briefcase. No, he had taken the only one. He went back to the briefcase, opened it and looked more closely. Like many expensive briefcases, there were many compartments. He inspected every one. Nothing. Frustrated, he picked it up and flung it across the room. It landed on its side. Dick sat on the floor to think and put his head in his hands. Had Ricky been faking? Did he know Dick was an imposter? Was there another briefcase? He lifted his head and stared at the briefcase. From this angle, it looked wide. He brought his hand up and hit himself in the forehead. No! It couldn't be. How could he have missed it? He scurried over, grabbing and opening it at the same time. A false bottom! He rushed back to the exam room, where he grabbed the first instrument he saw on the tray. It was a scalpel. He placed the case on the counter and used the scalpel to pry at a corner and sure enough, there was another compartment that he had missed. Finding the hidden latch, he popped it. The entire bottom portion contained two cushioned jewelers' trays covered in velvet cloth, which he removed from one. He was staring at six rows of about 30 polished diamonds of increasing size and luster.

Holy shit, he thought, I've hit the mother lode! He examined the other tray, which was equally impressive. With a whistle, he shook his head. Finally he thought. He looked at his watch. It showed 12:30. Not much time but enough. He carefully replaced the diamonds in the case, closed and locked it. Now, back to his patient.

Dick returned to the exam room where Enrique Hernandez, the mastermind of the ultimate money scam that had bilked hundreds of Dick's countrymen out of their life savings, lay sleeping peacefully. He thought about reviving him and bringing him back to justice in Costa Rica but that was not his job. His job was about recovering the money, which he'd just about done. That was enough. The investors, including him, would be happy just to get their money back. Then he thought about the other investors. What would they get? Well, they'll get the opportunity to present papers and get back a percentage of their investments after the backers of this operation got their full share. This is crazy. Banks, what are you thinking?

You don't change the mission in the middle of an operation! He just wanted to change clothes, give Ricky another knock out shot, grab that case and get out of Dodge. So why wasn't he moving? Damn! A part of him needed to give those other investors some closure. It was tempting. He could bandage Ricky up, keep him in a semi-conscious state and transport him back with the diamonds. He had enough sedatives and drugs.

No, it's not his job. He changed clothes, started gathering up his gear but something made him look at Ricky again. A moan or some kind of stir but he knew that Ricky would be coming out of it soon. He could give him a knock out shot or he could give him some pills that would make him a co-operative prisoner. Damn! He put his stuff down. He noticed the bandages on the counter. He could not only disguise Ricky but he could keep alive the idea within Ricky's mind that he would soon have a new face. Dick grabbed the bandages and started applying them to the face of Costa Rica's most notorious white-collar criminal ever. Done, he stepped back and admired his work. The facemask made Ricky look like the invisible man. Dick had left openings around the eyes and mouth.

Now, he was ready, here goes Dick thought. He gave Ricky a nudge on the shoulder.

"Mmm, huh? Que?"

"Ricky, wake up it's Dr. Golightly. We have to get you to a hospital. There were complications. They have the equipment we need. There isn't a moment to lose."

Ricky sounded frightened when he mumbled, "What? What kind of complications? Am I going to be ok? What about Maria?"

"Take it easy. I am just being cautious. You might have a problem with infection. Here, take these, they will help with the infection. Maria's fine, no complications, she's resting comfortably. She'll be fine," Dick said as he handed him two pills and a cup of water.

Ricky took the pills. In a couple of moments, he would be a co-operative and willing patient. Dick glanced at his watch. It was almost 1:00.

Chapter 34

12,000 FEET UP

Donny, who had been daydreaming, was shaken out of his thoughts by the crackle of the radio. "Five minutes to target. Get ready Donny," the pilot barked.

Donny gave him a terse, "Roger that," then gave Carlos and Frank a hand signal. The plane was banking. Donny knew that the pilot would soon cut his engines, which would be the signal for the three of them to bail. Carlos was at the door getting it open and securing it for the jump into the night sky. Donny looked out the window but all he could see was black. As the pilot came out of his turn, he caught the moon and now he could see the reflection of the moon on the lake. It was beautiful, Donny thought. He glanced at Frank who looked uncertain. Donny reached over and squeezed his shoulder and smiled. Frank returned his smile and gave him thumbs up signal. Donny gave him a quick pat on his back and signaled him to line up behind Carlos.

The three of them were now positioned. Carlos would be first out with Frank following him and Donny would bring up the rear. Donny caught a signal from Carlos who was pointing down and ahead. Donny looked down and there was the island, lit up like a Christmas tree. He could make out the castle. It looks like a scene from a kid's model rail set, Donny thought.

He was brought out of his thoughts by the cough and sputter of the engine. He looked over to see Carlos positioning himself like a cat ready to pounce. At the moment the engine died and there was silence, Carlos leapt into the night. Without hesitation, Frank followed a second later. Donny was right behind him. They floated in silence and concentrated on the target. Carlos led them on a dive to the east, which was the direction of the island. When he pulled up, they all did. Carlos gave a hand signal indicating that he would pull his cord first, Frank second and Donny last. With that, Carlos' chute popped and he rose up from them. A couple of seconds later, Frank did the same and then Donny.

Donny looked down. Below he could make out Carlos and Frank in the moonlit night steering their chutes this way and that. The castle loomed below them, its courtyard growing bigger by the second. Damn, I hope the guards are sleeping or not out in the open where they would see or hear three nutcases landing in their midst, Donny thought. He admired Carlos' skill as he expertly maneuvered his chute onto the target. Frank was a little off course but struggled to bring his rig back. Donny could see that Frank would be ok, so he concentrated on his own descent as he fought an unforeseen gust of wind. Just as he got it under control, he noticed that Carlos was about to land dead center and Frank was about to land off to the right. There was some kind of activity to the right. A guard has spotted them! The guard was pointing his weapon upward at Frank. Before he could get a round off, the guard froze and slumped to the ground. Now the guard was motionless and flat on his back. As he landed, he saw Carlos rushing towards the figure. The last thing they needed was an injured guard alerting the others. Carlos reached the body and felt for a pulse. Finding none, he promptly retrieved the dagger he had accurately thrown while in the process of landing his chute. He dragged the body to the nearest door. Opening it, he discovered it was a service closet. He put the corpse in the closet, covered it with his chute and closed the door. He went to rejoin the others who had already disposed of their chutes and were now hiding in the shadows of the alcove opposite the elevator.

Donny held his finger to his mouth indicating he wanted silence. He listened for the signal they had pre-arranged with Julio. They heard a bird call that the Nicaraguan guerrillas used to use when the country was at war. Chirp, chirp, chiiiirp. Donny stepped out of the shadow and immediately saw Julio who had emerged from the alcove that led to the elevator. Donny had his weapon at the ready and started to bring it up when Julio whispered, "Señor Donny? Don't shoot. It is me, Julio." Donny relaxed, stepped forward and shook Julio's out stretched hand.

"You must hurry, Senor, we are late. The other guards, they will come to relieve the ones who are on duty soon. Come with me, please."

With that, he turned to the elevator.

Donny signaled for Frank and Carlos to follow. The elevator was too small for all of them, so Donny told Frank and Carlos to take up positions in the shadows closest to the elevator alcove and wait for them to return.

CHAPTER 35

ESCAPE FROM THE ISLAND

Donny and Julio were at the entrance to the master suite in no time. Julio knocked once. They were fifteen minutes late but the door opened immediately. When Dick saw Donny standing there with Julio, he let out a huge sigh of relief and gave Donny a big ear-to-ear grin.

"I've seen that grin before. Does it mean you found the package, old man?" Donny asked.

"And a good evening to you too, Donny," Dick said with a smile. "Yeah, I've got what we came for indicating the briefcase on the table."

"*Señores*, we don't have much time. The guards, they will come. We must hurry. *Por favor!*" Julio said with urgency.

"Ok, Dick you ready?"

"Almost, here help me get a coat on him."

Donny looked at Dick like he was from another planet and said, "Are you crazy? We can't take him."

"Too late, I've made a decision. Besides, we don't have time to argue. Let's roll."

"You're gonna be the death of me." Donny said as he helped Dick finish dressing the criminal with Julio pleading with them to hurry all the while. Finally, they were ready. Dick grabbed the briefcase and stuffed the gun

Donny had given him into his pants. Julio checked the corridor, and seeing it was clear signaled for them to move out. Just as the elevator doors opened, a guard approached but before he could get a question out, Donny shot him without hesitation. The silenced Beretta had done its work. Dick held the door while Donny and Julio hid the body in a utility closet. They then descended to the courtyard level, where Frank and Carlos were waiting.

"Here," Dick said as he passed Ricky to Frank, "You handle him, I've had it with him."

"Sure Dick. Anything I should know?"

"Yeah. You just got your exclusive. Don't screw it up."

Frank looked puzzled but nodded.

"Ok, Julio, let's get to the boat," Dick said.

With Julio leading, they made their way down the stairs adjacent to the elevator. They couldn't use the elevator because the sound of its descent would alert the guard that someone was coming down. Once downstairs, they were in the cave-like alcove that Dick remembered from his arrival that seemed like days ago. Julio held up his hand. He whispered to Dick that he would go ahead and take care of the guard. He adjusted his uniform and casually strolled out of the alcove. He was just another guard arriving early to relieve his comrade. Dick wanted to see this, so he told the others to wait and crept to the opening and peered around the corner.

He saw Julio walk up to the guard and offer him a cigarette. The other guard smiled and accepted it. After they lit up, they talked and joked. The guard looked at his watch and said something to Julio who shrugged. The guard seemed to accept this. He tossed the cigarette, unslung his assault rifle and handed it to Julio. As Julio was accepting it, his hands gripped the stock and the barrel and with a lightning fast move, the stock came up and caught the guard in his throat. The guard fell to the dock. Julio pulled his combat knife and finished him off without a sound. All this took about three seconds. Dick was impressed with Julio's combat skills.

Julio saw Dick and signaled him to move out of the alcove. Dick turned to Frank and the others and signaled for them to move out too.

While Dick and the others started boarding the swamp boat, Julio jumped on board the cigarette boat and immediately went to the engine compartment. He took out a screwdriver and seconds later there were sparks. He closed the hatch and sprung on board the swamp boat and immediately went to the control panel, took out a key and started the engine. The sound that followed caused Dick to signal Donny and his guy to take up firing positions in case the other guards heard it. No one did. Just in case, Donny threw a smoke grenade into the elevator alcove and ran back down the stairs. Once on the dock, he immediately went to the cleats and untied the ropes holding the boat to its berth. They cast off. Julio put it in gear and as the boat moved away from the dock, Donny and Carlos jumped in. They headed southwest.

Everyone, with the exception of Enrique, was jubilant. Even Dick started to relax. Man, he could use a beer, he thought. The crowded boat moved steadily towards the southern shore. The moon had dropped considerably but it was still quite a sight as it reflected off the lake. Enrique was still like a drunk who had passed out. Dick checked, for the hundredth time that the briefcase was secure. Donny lay on one of the benches smoking and enjoying the night air. Frank, using the light from the moon was writing in his journal. Carlos sat motionless staring straight ahead.

Dick whispered to Donny. "What's with Carlos? He looks a little uptight."

Donny looked up just in time to see Julio coming up behind Frank with the butt of his rifle starting to come down on Frank's neck.

"Watch out!" Donny shouted but too late. The rifle butt found it's mark and Frank was sent sprawling to the deck face down.

Julio pointed his rifle at the group and reached for the case next to Dick. Julio was just coming to an upright position when he looked down with shock to see a knife in his chest. The ever-alert Carlos had thrown it with deadly accuracy. Donny scrambled to his feet and rushed to Frank's side. He was out. Donny slapped him gently trying to get him to come around. Donny, sensing something was wrong, looked up and noticed that no one was at the helm. He started barking orders.

"Dick, take the helm and make sure we're heading south. Carlos, keep an eye on Hernandez."

He went back to working on Frank. He was still unconscious but alive. There was nothing that he could do for him but make him comfortable which he did. Finished, he looked over at Julio who was flat on his back, his hand still clutching the briefcase. Donny pried the briefcase from his clenched hand and handed it up to Dick in the cockpit. He returned to the fallen guard and saw that he was alive, the Israeli combat knife still protruding from his chest. He's going to die, Donny thought.

Then he leaned over Julio and looked in his eyes and whispered, *"Porqué, Julio?"*

Julio looked up at Donny. With blood oozing from his mouth, he said *"Para Juanita y yo. Nosotros queriamos una nueva vida."* He had told Donny that he had done it so that he and Juanita could start a new life. I wonder if Juanita's in on it. He needed to find out.

"Juanita conoce esto?"

"No, Yo quiero sorprénderla."

He wanted to surprise her. Donny realized that it was just a spur of the moment action on Julio's part. Damn shame, Dick would have given Juanita and him somewhere in the neighborhood of a couple of grand. I guess Julio didn't realize that, he thought to himself. He looked down at Julio and saw that the kid was starting to slip. He put something under his head and held the kids hand and whispered words of encouragement in Spanish as Julio passed on. Donny gently covered Julio with some tarp and then turned his attention to his new friend and star student, Frank.

He grabbed Dick's medical bag and rummaged through it till he found what he thought to be smelling salts. He broke one and held it to Frank's nostrils. Frank reacted quickly and was soon asking what had happened. When he heard that Julio was dead, he sat up, looked around and said, "Donny, where are we?"

"We're ok. We're heading south from the island towards the southern shore where Miguel is waiting."

Dick who had evidently overheard said, "Damn. Julio knew the pick-up point. I'm not positive but I think it was southwest, not due south and not far from the island, about 25 miles."

CHAPTER 36

—————————— ■ ——————————

LOST AT SEA

Donny jumped up, went to where Dick was piloting the boat and told him to cut the engine. Puzzled, Dick complied. Once the engines were shut down, Donny looked at the compass on the small control panel. It was pointing south. He looked around. The moon had slipped behind clouds and it was much darker than it had been. The water was calm. He thought he could make out a light or two off to the right. He looked back at Dick and then at Frank and Carlos and said, "Does anybody know how long it's been since we left that dock?"

Carlos looked at his watch and said, "About a half hour, I think, Señor Donny."

Frank slowly picked himself off the deck and made his way over to the small cockpit area. Donny had found an ice pack in Dick's bag, which Frank held to his neck. As he approached the cockpit, he heard Dick say,

"Ok, let's not panic. According to Carlos, we've been traveling for about a half hour. How long ago was our little scuffle?"

"Maybe 15 minutes," Donny said.

"Ok, the boat does 12 knots an hour, that's about 13.5 miles per hour. According to your map, it's about 25 miles to the shore. Ok, that would put us four or five miles off the southern shore, but off course. Let me see that map of yours."

Donny handed him the map and after studying it, Dick started the engine and said, "We'll head west before heading south again. Everyone look for the lights of a small village that might be the town of Mexico."

Just outside the small town, Miguel had found a small rise overlooking the swamp that became the lake. He maneuvered the SUV where it was level and pointed it due north. While he waited, he thought about the money he would get from Dick for his part in the operation. He hoped it would be about five thousand, US but who knows, if things went off well, Dick might give him a bonus. In Costa Rica, that money would go far. He realized he'd been daydreaming. He looked at his watch. It was after 2:00am. He decided to start flashing his headlights once every two minutes.

As the boat moved west, all of them save Ricky who was once again out cold, were peering into to darkness of the shore. They had passed some lights but none that would qualify as a small village. It was Carlos who first spotted what turned out to be the lights of the town of Mexico. Everyone agreed that the lights they saw should be it, but it seemed so far away. Dick adjusted the course to a more southern direction and as they started to head in that direction, Frank saw the bright lights of the SUV flash on and off. He alerted the others and pointed to where he had seen the flash. Dick adjusted once again and picked up the speed a little to about six knots. The next time Miguel did it they all saw it, and Dick was ready with the swamp boat's powerful searchlight. He flashed it once, got a reply and headed towards the shore.

Miguel could see that they were tracking towards him. Taking the high beam emergency flashlight they had brought alone for precisely this purpose, he got out of the car and made his way down the embankment to the edge. Once there, he gave another flash and this time when the light from the boat responded, they could actually see Miguel on the bank. Dick slowed the boat and maneuvered it as close as possible. They might get their feet a little wet, Dick thought, but that was fine as they'd soon be inside the big SUV cruising towards San Jose.

Carlos got Ricky to his feet and helped him off like one would help a drunk. Donny helped Dick. Frank grabbed what was left of the gear. All shoes and boots were muddied up in exiting the boat but that was a small price to pay for getting out with their prize.

"Who's this?" Miguel said as pointed to Ricky.

"Extra baggage, put him in the rear cargo area. Don't worry, we'll pay for the extra baggage, *Señor Taxista,*." Dick said with a smile.

With that, Miguel winked and rushed ahead to open the rear cargo door of the SUV. Carlos followed and without ceremony, Dumped Ricky who was once again out cold, into the back.

Dick held a firm grasp on the briefcase. Miguel offered to take it. Dick almost growled as he told Miguel that he would hold on to it.

Loaded, Miguel expertly backed the big vehicle up to where he could turn around. The road, if you could call it that, was rough and full of water and mud. Dick thought they would have been better off using the boat here.

They finally emerged from the swamp and headed towards the town. Just before entering the town, they rounded a curve and ran straight into a Nicaraguan Border Patrol roadblock.

"Donny, give Miguel some of that bribe money. About two of the hundreds should do it," Dick said.

Donny slipped him the bills.

"Let Miguel do all the talking. He's had experience with these people."

The roadblock the Nicaraguans had set up consisted of a Land Rover with two soldiers. One of the soldiers, using the vehicle as a shield was pointing a rifle at them. The other approached the driver's side window with his pistol drawn. Miguel lowered the window and put his hands on the steering wheel so the soldier could see clearly see them.

"*Su pasaporte por favor,*" the soldier said. He sounded bored and sleepy.

"*Si*", Miguel said with a smile as he handed him the passport with the Ben Franklin's barely peeking out.

The soldier palmed the money, gave a cursory glance to the document, shined his flashlight into the vehicle then stepped back and told Miguel to move on. Just another day at the office in Central America, Dick thought.

Two hundred dollars to a Nicaraguan soldier was like a couple of thousand to a US border guard. The soldier and his *compadre* would party tonight, Dick thought as Miguel put the car in drive and slowly moved out.

The plan was to drive south to the town of Cañas where they would pick up CR 2, the Autopista that would take them to San José. Miguel looked at his watch. It was just after three in the morning. With a little luck, and if he made good time, they would just miss the morning traffic jam into San José.

They did make good time. They reached the Autopista in record time and just as they were getting on it, they heard a moan from the back. Ricky was coming around again. Although he had more pills, he told Donny to get in the back and tie him up and gag him. The ever-eager Donny climbed in the back and took care of business none too gently.

Dick asked if he could use Miguel's cell. He dialed information and got the number for Delta Airlines. He called Delta and made a booking for their flight to Atlanta the next morning. From Atlanta, he would connect to Amsterdam on KLM's evening departure.

After he made his booking, Frank asked what was going on.

"Just made reservations to go to Amsterdam tomorrow. A contact from my DEA buddy put me in touch with a jewelry broker there. I need to convert the diamonds to cash as soon as possible."

"Then what," Frank asked.

"Marvin set up an account with Scotiabank to cover our expenses. I'll have the money deposited to that account and be back in Costa Rica in a couple of days."

"And?" Frank asked as he continued to write in his journal.

"And, when we get back to San José, you and Donny get with Vito and Marvin. Start calling the investors who financed our little operation. Set up a meeting at the Colonial. I figure it should be in about five days from now. Tell them to bring evidence of their original deposits with the Cousins."

They all turned to look back as they heard groans and squeal like sounds coming from the rear. Enrique Hernandez who had evidently overheard the conversation was beet red as he tried to scream out to protest.

The laughter that erupted in the SUV went on for what seemed like forever. The distraction allowed Dick to quickly open the briefcase and extract something out of it. After closing the case, he looked around to make sure no one had noticed. He then fished in his pocket and pulled out a small envelope into which he slipped an object. Then he said, "Hey Frank, let me take a look at that journal. I want to check it for accuracy."

"What, you're an editor now?" Frank said but reluctantly handed it over.

Dick made a show of studying it while palming the envelope and slipping it into one of the back pages. He quickly closed the notebook and handed it back to Frank saying, "Looks fine to me, sport. By the way, how's the headache."

Frank just looked at him, accepted the book and said he would be fine.

Dick smiled and turned back to face the road.

CHAPTER 37

SAFELY HOME

Once they arrived in San José, it was decided that because of being foreigners in a foreign land, and not at all familiar with the intricacies of Napoleonic law that they would simply drop Senor Enrique Hernandez on the doorstep of Police headquarters in the Judicial Plaza. In Costa Rica, it is not uncommon for the police to arrest everyone involved in a criminal case and throw the whole bunch in jail while the investigation is completed. There have been cases where innocent persons have languished in the infamous San Sebastian prison for up to two years before things were sorted out in a court of law.

Additionally, they weren't at all concerned that any story Hernandez might tell would be believed. The only person he could possibly identify was Dr. Eric Golightly who would be released later this morning by Nicaraguan Immigration and sent back to Los Angeles without any explanation. The story he would tell would be too outrageous for anyone to believe. So, they simply dropped Ricky, still bound and gagged with a note on his chest on the front steps of the Police headquarters building and sped away. They figured they would read about it in *La Nación* the next morning.

They went next to Wally's apartment where they cleaned up and disposed of any remaining equipment or evidence as the police might call it. Wally got on the phone and before long, the others started showing up. When Juanita arrived, Dick pulled her to one side and told her the tragic news about Julio. She was saddened but understood what they had done and why. Dick was convinced that Julio had acted alone and gave Juanita her payment. Juanita cried, but was happy to get the money.

Marvin and Vito came together and were jubilant. They wanted to know all the details and pestered Frank and Dick until they spilled everything. Marvin wanted to see the diamonds. Reluctantly, Dick opened the briefcase on Wally's dining room table. Everyone gathered around to look. They were amazed at the size and luster of what lay in front of them. Marvin reached for one of the diamonds and Dick slapped his hand telling him to look but not touch. They all laughed. Everyone was jubilant. They had actually pulled it off! They toasted each other with cold beers over and over.

After the commotion died down, Dick told them that he would be leaving the next morning to convert the diamonds to hard cash which would be transferred to the Scotiabank account Marvin had set up. He told them he would be back by Friday and Wally, Marvin and Vito should call the investors and tell them to be at the Colonial Sports book for a meeting Saturday morning.

Before leaving, Dick gave Donny two envelopes, one for him and one for Carlos. Dick told Donny not to open his 'til tomorrow morning. Donny looked at him quizzically but agreed to honor Dick's request. As they left, Dick heard Donny tell Carlos that they better hurry, as the lunch buffet at the Casino Tropical would be over soon. Dick shook his head and told Miguel that he needed to go home, rest and pack. Dick asked Juanita to come with him. They piled into the SUV that Miguel would later return to the rental agency. In front of Dick's house, they shook hands and Dick told Miguel that he would have a special envelope for him tomorrow morning when Miguel picked him up at five am to go to the airport. Miguel grinned from ear to ear and hugged Dick. They bid each other farewell and as Dick and Juanita went up the walk, Miguel heard Juanita tell Dick that she wanted to give him a nice massage. Miguel smiled to himself as he pulled away.

The next morning, Dick awoke to the smell of fried eggs and Gallo Pinto beans expertly prepared by the beautiful Juanita who served them to Dick in bed. He felt refreshed and alert. After a thorough massage by Juanita the night before, he was feeling much better. When he came out of the shower, she was standing there naked with a fresh cup of coffee. Dick put the coffee on the bathroom counter and took Juanita into his arms. They hugged and before he knew it, Dick was aroused. They wound up back in bed and enjoyed a morning delight. Then they both went back to the warm shower where they bathed each other and giggled like children.

Miguel was right on schedule. Dick bid farewell to Juanita telling her to take another taxi to the airport and to meet him near the entrance but to stay out of sight till she was sure he was alone.

Since they were ahead of time, Miguel made a quick detour and stopped at the lot of an all-night auto broker who specialized in imported cars from Korea. Once there, Miguel showed Dick two late model KIA's he had put a deposit on the day before. Dick congratulated him on his choice and Miguel told him that he intended to form a new taxi company to compete with the three big companies in San Jose. Knowing Miguel, he'll make it, Dick thought. He reached in his coat pocket and pulled out a big envelope handed it to Miguel and asked him not to open it 'til he got home. Then he looked at his watch and told Miguel they would have to hustle. Since the broker's lot was near the airport, they made it in with time to spare. Miguel kidded Dick about looking nothing like the doctor he had dropped off at the same spot a couple of days ago. Dick got out of the taxi laughing.

He waved goodbye to Miguel who watched as Dick went across the glassed- in sky bridge that led to the ticketing area. He noticed a smartly dressed woman approach Dick and give him a kiss. Strangely, the woman bore a strong resemblance to Juanita. No, it couldn't be, Miguel thought. They had just left her at Dick's casa. It has to be just another one of Dick's many female admirers. Miguel just shook his head and laughed as he put the taxi in gear and pulled away from the curb.

Epilogue

————————————■————————————

As Miguel was pulling away from the airport, Donny was waking up with a major hangover. The free buffet had led to a round at the tables, which led to another round and before he knew it, he had picked up some lovely he had met and they must have come back to his place. He knew that because she was still in the bed with him. Man, she looked good, he thought. What was her name? Jennifer? Maria? He resisted an urge to wake her for a little morning sex but reluctantly got out of bed. He stumbled into the kitchen and made coffee. While he was waiting for the coffee to brew, he glanced around and saw the envelope Dick had given him the day before with instructions not to open it 'til this morning. Hell, it's morning, he thought as he sat down and tore it open. Inside there was a folded up piece of paper. When he took it out of the envelope, he felt something small and hard. He carefully unfolded the paper and a small bright diamond fell out onto his table. He picked it up and inspected it. It must be at least eight carats, he thought. Letting out a low whistle, he picked up the note. It was from Dick,

> *Donny,*
>
> *Good morning, amigo. I hope the enclosed didn't shock you too much. It should fetch enough to cover the minimum investment you made with the Cousins and then some.*
>
> *I also gave Miguel envelopes to give to Marvin, Vito and Wally. They too will receive enough to cover their losses.*
>
> *Please don't try to track me down. You know enough to know that a move like that could be hazardous to your health.*
>
> *Have a great life mi amigo. Pura Vida!*
> *Dick*

Donny laid the note down and carefully picked up the diamond. As he was inspecting it, a smile spread across his face. Aloud, he said, "You are one cool customer, Dick Banks."

Across town, Miguel arrived at his casa where his wife hugged him and told him to sit at the kitchen table while she started fixing him his breakfast. He took out the big envelope Dick had given him. As soon as he opened it, he saw why it was so big. Inside, he found four other envelopes. One addressed to him, one to Marvin, one for Vito, and one for Wally.

He opened the one addressed to him. Inside, he found a stack of one hundred dollar bills. It was a pretty thick stack he thought as he started counting. Before he got past four or five, he heard a gasp behind him. He turned to see his wife standing frozen behind him with her eyes wide open and her hand to her mouth. He laid the money down, got up and gave her a hug. He reassured her over and over that the money was earned honestly, and did his best to calm her down. After a while, she did and he was able to resume counting. He had expected a bonus of about three or four thousand but was amazed to discover ten thousand American dollars. He was grinning ear to ear as he picked up the note from Dick. It read:

> Miguel,
>
> Well I hope you're not too surprised with your bonus. The job would have been impossible to pull off without your help. Your pilot and his plane turned out to be exactly what we needed. You were always there for me, amigo.
>
> Please deliver the other envelopes to Marvin, Vito, and Wally for me. All three can usually be found having breakfast at the Gran Hotel Costa Rica almost any morning.
>
> In the coming weeks, you'll hear a lot of horrible things about me. Please don't think too badly of me. A man's got to do what a man's got to do.
>
> Pura Vida,
> Dick

Although he was a little confused by the last part, he was ecstatic about the money. He would now be able to get the two used taxis he had shown Dick earlier, and even have a little left over to buy his wife a washing machine which he knew she had wanted for years. He looked at his watch and made a quick decision. He would try and catch Marvin, Vito and Wally right now. He got up, gave his wife a kiss, told her to hide the money in a safe place and promptly left.

As he was leaving he heard his wife yelling, "But your breakfast, Mi Amor."

As soon as he pulled up to the hotel's area reserved for taxis, he spotted the three gringos sitting at their usual table joking and ogling the good looking tica secretaries on their way to work. They all were glad to see him and invited him to sit down which he did. He smiled and pulled out his big envelope. Then he gave each one of them a marked envelope and sat back to watch as they eagerly tore them open. Each received a diamond or diamonds of various sizes depending on what they had invested with the Cousins. They each also had a note from Dick expressing his thanks and asking for their forgiveness. Miguel watched as a look of bewilderment came over their faces. Then resignation. Then wide grins as everything set in.

Frank had begged off on joining them for breakfast. He had work to do. He had called Grimes in New York and gave him a quick rundown on the events of the previous few days. Grimes congratulated him and asked him to get a first installment to him as soon as possible as he wanted to make the late edition deadline.

Sitting in front of the laptop, Frank opened his notebook and started reading his notes. As he was turning pages, he thought he saw a bulge near the back of the notebook. He turned a few pages ahead. He then realized that the bulge was caused by a small envelope. He picked the envelope up and tore it open. He was amazed to find a diamond inside. He picked it up and inspected it. It was huge. Frank thought it must be worth quite a lot. He thought about it for some time and finally came to the conclusion that he would talk to Dick about it on Saturday. With that, he went back to work. He had a deadline to make.

About the same time his former friends were opening their envelopes, Dick and Juanita were clearing U.S. Customs in Atlanta. After they were cleared through and had re-checked their bags for the connecting KLM flight, Dick looked at his watch and told Juanita that, since they had three hours, they should go to the Crown Room as Dick had some calls to make. Once in the lounge reserved for First Class International passengers, Dick found a quiet phone area where he could make his calls in private. Juanita went to the bar and got them drinks.

His first call was to the extension of Frank Sommers at his office in New York. Dick knew that Frank would be checking his messages once he finished filing his story, so he left a message:

> "Hi, Frank.
>
> Hope you head is feeling better. With your inquiring mind, I'm sure that by now, you've come to the conclusion that I'm a scoundrel. Well, you're right. I am. My conscience did bother me enough to make sure my closest friends were taken care of. By now, I'm sure you found a little something extra in your notebook. If not, I'd check near the back of it. Anyway, it should fetch enough for you to quit that grind in New York and move to Costa Rica. I know the Tico Times would be interested in someone like you. Especially after you write about our little caper. I'll be checking the international editions of all the stateside financial papers for your award winning exposé. Enjoy the Pulitzer, amigo.
>
> Pura Vida!"

Smiling, he hung up and lifted the receiver for another call. This time it was to the offices of a renowned plastic surgeon in Geneva, Switzerland. He spoke briefly with the receptionist. He made an appointment for him and Juanita for the coming Monday.

He said, "Yes, we'll be flying in from Amsterdam Sunday, so we'll see you at nine on Monday morning?"

"Very good, monsieur, the doctor will see you both at nine."

He thanked her, hung up the phone, looked at Juanita, took a sip of his drink and with a wink said, "How's your French, mi amor?"

Made in the USA
San Bernardino, CA
11 July 2014